GLORIANA

Book Three of the 'Elizabeth I' trilogy, following THE RED-HAIRED BRAT and ABSOLUTE ELIZABETH.

For four days, the great Gloriana has remained huddled and silent upon a mound of cushions at Richmond, refusing to take to her bed, fighting death to the end. Memories crowd her brain: scenes of glory, scenes of power, times too, of alarm and dismay. Illustrious figures pass before her inward eye — the mighty Lord Burghley, beloved Leicester, cunning Walsingham, gallant Raleigh, handsome Kit Hatton. There, also, is her life's bane, Queen Marie of Scotland. There is wild, foolish Essex, Drake the explorer, Hawkins, Frobisher, Philip of Spain, conniving cousins, and comradely cousins. But Elizabeth's hand is steady upon her England until she breathes her last.

Books by Joanna Dessau
Published by The House of Ulverscroft:

THE GREY GOOSE
THE BLACKSMITH'S DAUGHTER
CROWN OF SORROWS
NO WAY OUT
THE CONSTANT LOVER
TAKE NOW, PAY LATER
ALL OR NOTHING

ELIZABETH I TRILOGY:
THE RED-HAIRED BRAT: BOOK 1
ABSOLUTE ELIZABETH: BOOK 2

JOANNA DESSAU

◆

GLORIANA

Complete and Unabridged

ULVERSCROFT
Leicester

First published in Great Britain
under the title of
'Fantastical Marvellous Queen'

First Large Print Edition
published 2000

British Library CIP Data

Dessau, Joanna
Gloriana.—Large print ed.—
Ulverscroft large print series: general fiction
1. Large type books
I. Title
823.9'14 [F]

ISBN 0–7089–4228–8

Published by
F. A. Thorpe (Publishing)
Anstey, Leicestershire
Set by Words & Graphics Ltd.
Anstey, Leicestershire
Printed and bound in Great Britain by
T. J. International Ltd., Padstow, Cornwall

This book is printed on acid-free paper

TO THE MEMORY OF MY
HENRY

Prologue

RICHMOND PALACE
17th March 1603

Sad, weary and feared am I. A great Queen should not be, but sad, weary and most desperate feared am I. Weary because I am old, sad because my dear, dear Kate, my cousin's child, my friend, my relative, has died, and feared because I feel in my aged bones that I shall follow her all too soon. Christ, but I do not want to die, I cannot, will not die. Others might fade and fall from the stem of life, but not Elizabeth Tudor. Nay and nay!

Oh, but I am unwell! My cold has come upon me again; I cannot sleep for restless fidgetings and the rheumatic pains in my arm. There is a burning in my breast and my mouth is parched with a thirst that no drink can slake. Mayhap the torrent of tears I shed for Kate dried up all the moisture in me. I became ill on the last day of February and since then have been unable to regain my spirits. Now a fever is upon me and a terrible heaviness of mind. There is only Philadelphia

1

left, Kate's sister, and she was never so close to me in love or understanding. Even she knew me not in my prime. She is dear and kind, but it is not the same.

Young Robert Cecil has been at me to take to my bed, but that I will not do. Nay, to go to bed is to admit that I am truly ill, and sometimes those who are truly ill are like to die. Ah God, to die! 'Tis fearful thought, dread imagination. I cannot bear it. But indeed I am not strong enough to walk about, or even to stand for long, although I did stand for some hours, striving to hold sickness and weakness at bay. Then, tiring, I said I would sit upon cushions.

The cushions were brought, a pile of many coloured velvet and silken pillows, red, blue, purple, gold, violet; some broidered, some corded, and I sank upon them. That was four days ago and still I rest upon cushions, for to bed I will not go.

There seems to be no place for me now. Nay, not even in mine own realm, in mine own palaces. My people still love me, but I am old, I cannot move about as I did. My memory, that famed and mighty power, fails me at times, and there is no one left who loves me for myself. They are all dead and I am alone. Alone, old and sick with naught but older age and more infirmity to come.

Better, then, to die? Nay, I say, and nay! I must live, for I am mortal feared to die. No matter what says Archbishop Whitgift, my Little Black Husband, as I call him. No matter what he prates of God and Jesus and eternal glory in Heaven, how do we know, for sure, that it be true? None has returned to tell us of these joys, 'tis all hearsay when all is said and done. How do I know that I will receive these joys, if so they be? I am no saint, no tender, holy soul with a clear conscience and a guileless heart. Mayhap 'tis all sleep, never to wake again. A terrible thought to me who hates to waste a moment of living in sleep. What, never again to see my lovely England and smell the sweet earth after the rain; never again to watch the buds swell in spring, to see the roses bloom in June and the leaves to fall wild and bronzen in the autumn?

And yet to live on, older, uglier and more sick — what a horrid choice have I! So I will not choose, I will leave it to God or fate as I have ever done when faced with a decision I cannot resolve. I will sit on my cushions and meditate until God shows His hand. There is much to meditate upon, i'faith. I have lived a long and full life for which I am thankful. I have known and seen and done much, some good, some bad. Ay indeed, ay, indeed.

Will I meet my cousin, Marie Stuart, when I leave this earth. I wonder? I never saw her in life, although she made life hard enough for me in her day. Will she have her head upon her shoulders when and if we meet? 'Tis wild and gloomy thought that, but I cannot put it from me. After she came into England, there to plague me, my peace of mind was gone for ever. Thirty-five years ago that was, and oh, what a mort of trouble burst upon my head. Ay, she set all by the ears wherever she went, did cousin Marie. I remember it as well as if it were but yesterday . . .

1

TREASON DOTH
NEVER PROSPER
1568 – 1572

Marie Stuart, Queen of Scotland, daughter of debate and douleur, came into England, unasked and unwelcome, in the tenth year of my reign. Dishonoured and defamed. She had abdicated in favour of her one-year-old son James. Her bastard half-brother, the Earl of Moray, was now Regent of the realm. My repose of mind was destroyed, for I knew that my northern Catholics would flock to her side if they dared. I knew that there was danger of a rebellion because of her. My life's bane she was, and so remained.

I was thirty-five years old at the time and still very handsome, looking far younger than my years and possessing great vitality of body and mind. My skin was snow-white, taut and unlined, my rich hair red as fire, my tall slender body lithe and athletic, my bosom high and firm as a girl's. My large amber eyes sparkled with animation, my long slender hands sparkled with jewels.

For public appearances I favoured brilliant colours encrusted with gems in order to be clearly seen by the populace. In private I preferred loose gowns of soft silky fabrics in subtle shades, for I well knew what suited me and how to make the best of myself.

My beloved Robert Dudley, now Earl of Leicester, whom I would have married had I a mind to wed, why, I loved him all my life in my fashion. We belonged together, he and I, for we shared the same birthdate and birth year. Our destinies were thus bound and so were our hearts. He was beautiful; tall, with a proud, hawk-like countenance, aquiline like mine own, but as dark as I was white and fair. We had known one another from childhood when he was a younger son of haughty John Dudley, my father's Lord Admiral, and I a poor little Princess, kept down, unwanted, unloved.

Now I was Queen, feted and loved by all. I pleased myself, I directed England's policies, I used myself as bait in the international marriage-market in order to gain allies, and I flirted outrageously with any gentleman who took my fancy. I spoke six languages fluently and used them all; I composed and played music upon the clavichord, I wrote verse, sang, danced, walked, hunted — oh, a fiery, dashing star in the worldly firmament was I! Some said the maidenliest, too, for I refused to marry, having no taste for the state through hard lessons learned in my childhood; because I wished to have no master and because my value as a marriageable woman, if I wedded, would be lost, and with it my use to England. My feelings were none so maidenly, for I had a passionate nature, but what would you, no one can have all she wants in this life, even so be she a Queen. Indeed, I was the anachronism of my day, a woman with political genius — the mind of a man 'twas said. But it was my woman's spirit and fascination that beguiled 'em, and much was I excused because of it. I could weep and show temper and petulance, I could be moon-moody, blow hot, blow cold, and all was forgiven me because I was a woman.

I had been beginning to feel that all was steady under my hand when Marie Stuart tumbled into England and put me out of quiet for years. I had a great quarrel with good William Cecil, my trusted Secretary of State, over her future. Cecil saw her as a disgrace to Scotland and her crown, an adulteress, a murderess, a threat to Protestantism and a threat to me. He wished her sent back to her mountains for her half-brother, Lord Moray, to do as he would with her. I could not agree to this. She was my kinswoman, royal and a Queen in her own right. Although dishonoured, her status had been equal to mine own. Higher, she would have said! I could not dispose of her as if she were an unwanted piece of baggage, though indeed I wanted her not.

Sir Francis Knollys my Vice-Chamberlain, and Baron Scrope my Warden of the Western Marches, I sent to Carlisle to welcome her officially. They were charmed by her, writing in fulsome fashion of her sweetness and grace. She had full measure of those qualities, for all I knew who met her said the same, but such qualities do not make a ruler. Sir Francis wrote me that she had cut off all her hair in order to effect a worthy disguise for her escape; he seemed very sorrowful over it, and sure, it was a great sacrifice, for she was famed for her hair. It never grew back properly after, I heard, forcing her to take to wigs to cover her loss.

However, it was not long before his letters began to take a different turn, seeming somewhat less enthusiastic, mentioning her 'violent appetite' and how that all deeds were no deeds with her unless that appetite were fulfilled. She appeared to be setting Carlisle by the ears and becoming a perilous nuisance there, so I had her transferred to

Bolton Castle under the care of my cousin Duke Norfolk's sister. I promised that she should be treated according to her station, warning her not to seek help from abroad and to remain quiet, but I felt that there was scant chance of her quietude, or of her restraint from seeking foreign assistance. A canker, a boil, a sore, a splinter in my flesh she would be — I knew it. A very lodestone to draw troubles and plots to her as bees to honey, oh I was saddled with her now, and what would come of it I could not tell.

While Sir Francis was in Carlisle with Queen Marie, his wife my beloved cousin Katey died. She was daughter to my mother's sister, Mary Boleyn, and I loved her most deeply, feeling distraught and bereft without her. A dreadful loss indeed, for although I did not love easy, I loved well, and Katey had been very close kin, so gentle, so dear. It would be desperate hard for Sir Francis to return home thus bereaved. She went too sudden for him to have been recalled to London over such a long journey; it was right sorrowful and I wept many tears for his affliction and mine.

Before two se'enights were fairly out, Marie's Ambassador, Lord Herries, came to me with a request from his mistress that he should be let go to France for help, since England refused it. I received him in my small Audience Chamber with Cecil, Rob and some other Privy Councillors at hand, for this was official business. I could not grant his request.

'Indeed not, my Lord,' I said, striving to keep the indignation from my voice. 'I am not so bereft of my senses as to allow your Queen to let the French into my country! I forbid it.'

'Well then,' he ventured, 'would your Majesty be willing to send an army into Scotland to restore my Queen to her throne?'

'I would not,' I replied, 'and shall not do so. I wonder that you and your mistress should think of such a thing, and you may tell her so. I cannot embroil my country in a war, which is what such an action would mean.'

What a fix I was in! Through my impulsive promise, earlier, to aid Queen Marie, I had, in Archbishop Parker's words, 'taken the wolf by the ears'. I had done my best, against all counsel, to help her to regain her throne; I had quarrelled with all my ministers and driven my devoted William Cecil near demented over it, and although her throne was indeed lost, 'twas only through my intervention that her life was not lost also. Now I was being made to seem unfeeling and cruel by having to refuse these unallowable entreaties. It was too bad. Hardly waiting for Lord Herries to back out of the door. I was on my feet, marching across the room and calling to my ladies to dress me in my riding habit. I took a goodly gallop, alone but for a groom, cross-country to Chelsey Village and back by way of the Knight's Bridge over the Westbourne River, returning to White Hall, heated, but in a better frame of mind.

This was speedily put to flight by the arrival of a letter from Marie asking me to furnish Lord Fleming with a passport to France in order to negotiate with Catherine de' Medici on her behalf. After reading it, I threw it to the ground.

'What next?' I cried. 'Lord Fleming, a Scot and Governor of Dumbarton Castle, to go to France with my permission, to treat with my enemies for one whom I am fast being persuaded is also my enemy! Well, I shall not answer it and he shall not go.'

'She will not be satisfied with that,' said Mr. Secretary Cecil staring out of the open lattice at the sun-flecked water of the River Thames. I could hear the cries and shouts of those disporting themselves in boats, and the faint, reedy sound of a flute and singing far away. I wished I were so carefree. 'She will demand an answer,' declared Cecil.

She did. Soon enough came another letter, couched in more forcible terms. I was astounded at such effrontery, and wrote a trenchant reply, begging her to have some consideration for me, her reluctant hostess, instead of always thinking of herself. 'Twas doing so had lost her her throne, that was sure. And as for me, every decision I made hereafter would be disapproved by someone. I could not be right in it, no matter what I did. In my heart, I wished her well out of the way, but she was a Queen in her own right, and I believed, with all that was in me, that once a Sovereign be overruled or overpowered, no other Sovereign could be safe. I could not leave her to the angry Scots, my conscience would not allow me.

'But I cannot receive her officially, as she seems to think I should!' I protested to Cecil upon another fine and sunny day when all were outdoors but he and I. Nay, he and I were sitting at a table, chins on hands, our foreheads creased, as we sought for a solution to the problem. 'I cannot fight the Scottish rebels for her and restore her to her throne, when all believe she was a party to the murder of her husband — my relative by blood, incidentally! Then to marry the Earl of Bothwell, also suspected of the murder, and split Scotland in two — why the whole country has suffered for her follies. I cannot plunge England into such an affair. Besides, what of your Treaty of Edinburgh, Cecil?'

'She has not yet ratified it,' he said heavily.

'Nay, for to confirm it, she would have to give up her fancied right to the Royal Arms of England and recognise me as the true Queen of my own realm!' I retorted. 'You see what it is, Sir Spirit? She means to succeed me if she can, and take my place on the throne before that, if she dare. We must discover the truth of her conduct with Lord Bothwell over the murder of her husband. That is essential.'

'We could open an enquiry, Madam. To my mind, 'tis the only way, for neither the Lord Regent Moray or Queen Marie can manage without our help. It has come to that.' His keen, intelligent face was pale, the brilliant grey eyes full of care as they looked into mine.

'Well then, so we shall. See to it, my Spirit. I leave it to you to choose the time and place, but whatever falls out, I will act as arbiter in the matter. It is my place to do so. Indeed, I can do no less.'

He smiled. 'Yours is the hand of power, Madam. I will do as you wish.'

Of course, Marie was incensed at the mere

13

notion of an enquiry into her actions, but her position was such that she could not but agree. To have refused would have confirmed her guilt in the minds of all, although she intended to admit nothing, behaving throughout as if Lord Moray and his supporters were the defendants in a charge of rebellion against her, telling her agents, Lord Herries and the Bishop of Ross, to act in a like manner. 'Twould seem she had no fault at all! Well, we would find out.

The Commission of Enquiry opened on the 4th of October at York, presided over by my kinsman Tom Howard, Duke of Norfolk, the Earl of Sussex and little Sir Ralph Sadleir, a skilful diplomat and one of Cecil's most trusted men, who was said to know more about Scotland than any other Englishman.

The Regent of Scotland, Marie's dour, dark half-brother, wished to know if my English government would keep Marie a prisoner if he could prove that she had been implicated in the murder of her husband, Henry Darnley. Darnley had been my cousin Margaret Lennox's child, a nasty enough young man, with a taste for little boys in his bed and an inordinate amount of drink in his belly. As a husband he was no loss, but

14

his manner of going was disastrous. To be blown up with gunpowder, strangled and left dead and naked in a snow-covered field was his unfortunate fate. Marie would marry him, Christ alone knew why. I would not have touched him with a two yard pike. But she was no judge of men, nor of anything else, as it turned out to her unluck and mine.

Sussex and Norfolk told Lord Moray that his question must be referred to London, it being too hot a matter for them to handle, and rightly so. Then Moray spoke of how Marie had handed the ruling of Scotland over to the Earl of Bothwell, her next husband, and how all Scotland had been against such an action. So he spoke aloud, but privately he showed the Commissioners copies of certain letters which had been found in a silver-gilt casket under Bothwell's bed. The casket had been Marie's own, for it had belonged to her first husband, King François of France, and bore his initial and a crown. What careless folly! It beggared all belief. Marie and Bothwell were well-matched in that if in naught else.

After this, matters seemed to haver and hover in York, getting no forrader, until in exasperation at such cavilling behaviour, I ordered the whole Commission to London, to confer again at Westminster, for I sensed

15

some underhand work.

'It is too bad,' I said irritably to my loved Robert Dudley as we walked in the shrubbery, past the aviaries set up by my father. The wind had a sharp nip and the leaves blew about us in a tawny storm of colour. 'Here I am, back from Hampton, and all because of this damned Commission. I look forward to my autumn days at Hampton, thou knowest, away from noise and stinks. Some havey-cavey work is afoot. I feel it in my bones, Rob.'

'Plots, mean you, sweeting?' He looked concerned and anxious, his dark eyes troubled.

I patted his arm. 'Maybe. I feel uneasy about Norfolk, to tell truth.'

His hands clenched. 'That knave!' he exclaimed. 'I would not trust him, Bess. He is a conceited, jealous fool.'

'Ah well,' I laughed, 'he does not like you, does he? He thinks you arrogant and upstart, my darling. He thinks you treat me with too much familiarity in public — and in private,' I added making a kiss with my lips. Rob caught me in his arms and we exchanged several long and passionate kisses, but could not linger for 'twas too chill. After a while we continued our walking.

'Indeed, I am beginning not to trust

16

him,' I said. 'Cecil murmurs that he is bewitched by my Scottish cousin's rank and position; so much so that he cannot be totally unbiased.'

'You mean he would find in her favour?' Rob was incredulous.

'I do not know,' I answered, 'but Sussex and Sadleir would never agree to such a verdict, and that, mayhap, is why there is such a stalemate at York. I want you, my love, in your capacity as a Privy Councillor, in company with Cecil and the other Councillors, to act on the Commission with Norfolk, Sussex and Sadleir, and help to bring some commonsense to the business.'

He stopped, catching at my hands, my arms. 'Bess, darling Bess, will you not wed me? You have so much on your shoulders, you look a-weary and you have not been well. Let me protect and guard you, my dear one. I love you more than my life.'

I sighed, 'I know. And I love you.'

'Then will you not? I have waited so long and so patient.'

'Patient? You? Pigs might fly!' But I kissed him to show no unkindness meant.

He pushed me back against a tree, his knee between mine own, his hands on my breasts beneath the cloak, his mouth possessive on my eager lips. I could no more fight him

17

away than fight away my love for him, and we besported ourselves like any country couple, except for the chill and the lack of a comfortable couch. And, as usual, he did not get his way entire with me, but then he had given up hoping for that long ago, for I could not do it. It had become impossible for me to receive him fully as a woman does her lover. My body would not obey. So mayhap he was, after all, patient in his fashion.

'What mean you, I look a-weary?' I said as we began to return to the palace. 'Dost mean I look old, is that it?'

'Nay, sure not! I meant only that you have a look of care and you should not tire yourself after being unwell.'

'Jesu, that was only belly-gripes! Do you coddle me now, like some old grandam?'

'Well, it was pains in the face and neck before that.'

'Rob, you are worse than a nursemaid! Cease your fussings. That was the toothache and a stiffness in the neck caused by sitting in a draught. 'Tis naught, and I am one who recovers swiftly.'

'Oh ay. And your migraines? They are naught also, I suppose.'

'You have me there,' I confessed. 'They are a misbegotten plague indeed, but I have had them since a child, see'st thou, and I am

18

as used to them as I shall ever be. They are part of my life now. Forget it, Rob; let us think of pleasant things like a masked dance tonight, or kissing games. What say you?'

For answer, he whispered in my ear and I laughed aloud, for 'twas bawdy and concerned us both.

★ ★ ★

I had heard it whispered by Bertrand de Salignac de la Mothe Fénélon, the French Ambassador, that Duke Norfolk had the thought of marriage in his head. So Cecil, as ever, was right.

'Indeed!' I sniffed. 'And of whom is he thinking for a fourth wife, Monseigneur? Could it be a certain royal lady in the North?'

'*Bien sur, Majesté! La Reine Marie* is in his mind. *Le Duc*, he imagines to enlarge himself, to advance in the world, *voyez vous.*'

'He will be unlucky then,' I returned, 'for I mean to close the Commission at York and bring it down to Westminster where I can keep watch over what goes on. I have had my doubts about Norfolk for some time. I like not weak heads, greedy pockets and wavering loyalties. He will not enlarge himself at my

19

expense, I do assure you.'

I thought that Lord Moray, too, was taking his time over the business, devious creature that he was, so, acting swiftly, I had the whole Commission transferred then and there to Westminster, where it reopened in the Star Chamber on the 25th of November 1568.

As well as this, I had a tricky situation to handle in the matter of my Channel privateers. These bold sailors were almost all English and of good family, having taken to piracy as disallowed Catholics in my brother Edward's reign, or as equally unpopular Protestants in the time of my sister Mary. One John Hawkins, with a young cousin called Francis Drake, had even captured two Spanish ships as far abroad as Vera Cruz in the new land of Mexico. I turned a blind eye to all this — after all, a weak woman cannot have her watch upon everything that goes on outside her own kingdom — and found the rich spoils a goodly addition to my ever-hungry Exchequer. Besides, it were better than outright war with Spain, which is what would have occurred had I acknowledged the existence of my pirates. England was not yet ready for that.

There was much piracy, in fact, against the Spaniards in the Broad Ditch or Narrow Sea, names we have for the channel 'twixt England and France. There was also buccaneering along the coasts of France and the Netherlands. I could not be held responsible for the actions of other countries as well as my own, I told the enraged new Spanish Ambassador. Why did he insist that the pirates were all English? It seemed most unjust, I said, to blame England for every misdeed taking place beyond her shores!

Don Guerau de Spes was not to be so easily mollified, and appeared to have but little understanding of the weakness of womanhood, flushing darkly and breathing heavily through his nose as he bent his frowning gaze upon my guileless eyes.

'Dost realise, *Vuestra Majestad*,' he said, lapsing into rapid Spanish, 'that your pirates have put five Spanish ships to flight, forcing them to take refuge in English ports? They were but small cargo ships, not equipped for heavy warfare.'

'Dear me,' I replied in the same tongue, looking most concerned, 'is there much of value aboard, Ambassador?'

He swallowed and made a slight gobbling sound. 'Much of value? Merely the paltry sum of £85,000 lent to my master, King Philip, by Genoese bankers, *Majestad*!'

'Then what,' I asked, in the same innocent

manner, 'was it doing sailing about in the Channel?'

He shook his head in exasperation at the weak wits of this foolish woman who imagined she could rule a country by herself. 'The money is intended for Antwerp, to pay the soldiers of the army of the Duke of Alba, who, as your Majesty knows, is leading the Spanish forces in a war against the Netherlands. He needs the money, *Madonna*. Will you not see your way clear to provide an armed escort for the pay ships?'

I paused for a moment, looking puzzled. 'But surely,' I faltered hesitantly, 'surely this money is still the property of the Genoese bankers until it is actually delivered in Antwerp?'

He could not stifle a gasp. 'As to that — I — I am not certain, *Majestad*.'

'I believe you will find it so, Ambassador,' I said, smiling trustfully up at him. 'I am in an unfortunate situation myself, for my country is very short of funds because of the difficulties of trade with the Netherlands, due to Duke Alba and his war there. My customs revenue is greatly reduced thereby. I feel it only fair to tell you that I have been in touch with the Genoese bankers myself, over this money, and they have been kind enough to

22

transfer the loan to me, my need being so great.'

Lord, he near took an apoplexy at this, and no wonder, poor gentleman; 'twas delicious moment. But I had to exert all my diplomacy after, to avert a war with Alba over the matter. The luck was on my side, that after I had appropriated the money, Alba could not afford to take on England in battle. It was as simple as that. It was not all luck, see'st thou. I used my head to help it along. My head and Cecil's. Our minds were as one.

But it was a worrisome time, for all that, and I wondered that I retained my looks with so much as I had to fret over. My temper, never sweet, was certainly affected and I snapped and quarrelled with everyone. Man's brain or no, my nerves were always touchy. 'Twas no wonder after the youth I had suffered and the strains I had endured. One is not made of wood.

There was my cousin Norfolk; I had trusted him, been fond of him, allowed him great freedom of speech and frankness. He was next in rank and title to mine own, the first Duke in England. When he and the Commission came to London, I thought it fair to give him a warning as to his doings. 'Cousin,' said I, 'be seated here with me by the fire and tell me if what I hear is truth. Do you intrigue to wed the Queen of Scots?'

His glancing brown eyes shifted from mine, then stared back with a great assumption of innocence. 'Why Madam,' he exclaimed, 'no reason could move me toward the like of her that hath been a competitor to the Crown! I swear that if your Majesty should force me to do this, I would rather be committed to the Tower, for I never mean to marry with such a person, where I could not be sure of my pillow!' He was all noble indignance and it fooled me not one whit. He knew it too, and from then on became uneasy and strained in my presence, the cowardly fool, blaming Cecil for having told me of his secret plans.

Almost as soon as the Commission reopened, Moray produced those letters which had been found in the casket under Bothwell's bed, and accused his half-sister of murder. I, and all the officers, saw and handled them. There seemed no doubt that they were genuine; none questioned the fact, in spite of Queen Marie's flat denial of them, she saying that they were all forgeries. I begged her, in repeated letters, to make a formal repudiation, but this she refused to do unless her future be guaranteed. Arbiter of the proceedings though I was, I could not pronounce her innocent before the enquiry

24

be over! Nor could I pronounce her guilty, despite my feelings, for this would be to bring an anointed monarch down to the level of an ordinary criminal. If such a thing could happen to one Sovereign, it could happen to another. I wished to put no such thought in any mind, where I was concerned. I wanted naught to do with anarchy and wished to close the Commission as soon as possible for I was becoming right anxious about Norfolk.

He was causing much dissension by his behaviour, and, as far as I could tell, he had turned against my Cecil which was tantamount to turning against me, his Sovereign. Good Cecil had much respect for Norfolk's rank and was, even at that time, helping him in the knotty business of his Dacre stepdaughters. Norfolk had wedded Elizabeth Lelbourne, widow of Lord Dacre, who was already mother to three daughters and a son by her dead lord. The boy, George, a bright and active youngling, had so hurt himself in a fall from a vaulting horse that he had died of his injuries, leaving his sisters as great heiresses. Having much desire for wealth and riches, Norfolk was wishful to wed them all to young men of his own Howard family, but Lord Dacre's brother, Leonard, was opposing this plan with all his might, feeling that the title and estates should come to him. The final decision in this difficult affair was Cecil's, in his position as Master of the Wards, so it was idiotic of Norfolk to quarrel with a powerful would-be friend when so much was at stake in his fortunes. It was jealousy, see'st thou.

Rob, too, was fiercely jealous of Cecil and had always been so, envying his grasp of governmental politics and his closeness to me. It was no secret that Rob wished to climb higher and saw Cecil as a constant stumbling block. The block was not entirely Cecil, neither. Rob rated his powers high; higher than I rated them. I knew full well that his ideas were bigger than his capabilities in the tricky matter of statecraft, for all of his skill between the sheets of a fourposter, and I, though he realised it not, stood in his way also.

Norfolk and Rob had very little use for one another. Norfolk had always acted most arrogant towards Rob, saying aloud that he was not of the old nobility and that his father had been a resounding villain who had brought the country to its knees. True enough, but unnecessary to mention it. Rob had found it expedient to use his wits and charm to achieve his place and Norfolk despised such behaviour utterly, making it woundingly obvious to all the Court by his treatment of my dear Rob, criticising his manners and calling him 'upstart'. So there was no love lost between the two, making it all the more extraordinary that Norfolk should choose Rob as confidante in his plan to bring down Cecil. It seemed to me that he had lost all judgment and care of thought.

It was not Cecil's time of luck in these months. His stars were square against him, for he had become unpopular in the City too, for many of the smaller merchants had had their ships seized by Spain in reprisal for the little matter of Alba's pay money, over which Cecil had advised me so craftily. Sir Tom Gresham, our great financier, was firm behind him, as were the big merchant-men, but there was much dissatisfaction, nevertheless. As well as this, Cecil had devised a state lottery, a clever notion, the monies of which would go to repair harbours and finance public works. Unfortunately, fewer tickets were bought than hoped, and the funds that came in barely made up the amount of the proposed first prize. What a roar was there when the lots were drawn at the West Door of St. Paul's in January! Cecil was accused of lining his pockets with the missing monies, in furious terms. So nobles and commoners were against my poor Spirit at that time. In addition, Duke Norfolk had been borrowing heavily from an Italian banker named Roberto di Ridolfi, whom he and others thought to be an ordinary man of business. What they did not know was that Ridolfi's money for his 'business' came from the Pope and was to be used to cause dissension and unrest in England. Ridolfi was also in communication with the arrogant and unpleasant Spanish Ambassador, Guerau de Spes, telling him that Norfolk and Arundel were certain that they could overthrow my government and raise another with themselves at the head!

There was much that these pretty conspirators did not know; the most important being their ignorance of *my* knowledge of the whole affair. What! Did they think I slept? That I played at being Queen, that I heard little and saw less, like the Lady of Scotland? Nay, mine eyes and ears were everywhere. One cannot rule else. There was Fénélon who gave me hints, there was Cecil's aide, John Clapham, who knew all his master's secrets — oh, I had my sources. I would watch and wait till the time be ripe.

Upon Ash Wednesday, 22nd February, that time came. I had summoned a Council meeting to deal with this nasty matter and

28

allowed the Lords to wait for me. I stood, silent, listening outside the half-closed door of the Council Chamber, hearing the sounds within.

'Tear off his cap!' I heard, and 'Force him to his knees, the sneaking rat!' It was enough. Hurling the door wide, I swept into the room to see my Cecil held upon his knees by Norfolk and Arundel, his cap in Rob's hand, confusion and uproar all around. Hastening up to poor Cecil, I laid my hand on his shoulder.

'Up, my Spirit,' I said to him. 'Your quarrel is mine. Stand up now and go to thy place.' Then I rounded fiercely upon the plotters who looked most wretchedly dumbfounded. I gave them no more than a flick of my fingers and they scattered to all corners of the chamber, Rob fumbling desperately with the cap, finally laying it upon the table close to Cecil's hand.

Jesu, but I told them my feelings in the loudest and most forcible terms. 'Cowardly suckfists! Dolts! Slabberdegullions!' I shouted; words, which from any other than myself, would have had them all whipping out their swords. Ay, I let them have it finely. Rob came shamefaced to my side at once, Norfolk havered and gasped, the others stood downcast with naught to say. A disgraceful sight it was, and right disgusted was I that my Councillors should behave so.

So great-hearted was my Cecil that he said no more about this episode, keeping it secret and taking no advantage from it as well he could have done. It would have been bad for England, he said. Afterwards, however, he did take great pains to gain Council's approval for all his business as Secretary of State, but doing naught in the matter of revenge upon his would-be destroyers. He even held out the hand of friendship to Norfolk, wishing not to divide the realm.

Dear Tom Radcliffe, my good Earl of Sussex, was delighted at Cecil's forbearance, for although he had ever disliked poor Rob as an opportunist upstart, he had greatly admired Cecil and Norfolk. Until this sorry affair, Sussex had deemed Norfolk to be a true statesman above private inclines. Alas, 'twas no longer true, and Norfolk was henceforward to be enmeshed in greed, plots and private inclines to his life's end. By the July of 1569, I and all others at Court knew full well of his correspondence with Queen Marie and his desire to wed her. He was a poor one at keeping secret, having told Cecil, for one, of his hopes. To me he said no word, and Christ knows I gave him chance enough. But he was a greedy coward,

I fear, and double-tongued withal. Ha, when I think of the opportunities I made for him to confess to me! Why, I would have forgiven him could we have talked of it and made all clear between us.

There was the time in the little enclosed garden at Oatlands where the yew tree grows in the centre of four flower beds. The sun was shining and tiny pears and peaches appearing on the espaliered trees against the wall when Norfolk arrived from London. I sent for him to the garden to greet me there, in private, amongst the roses. I looked well enough, I recall, clad in a white satin gown trimmed with pearl, my hair dressed all over in curls, pearl entwined.

'Ho, cousin!' I greeted him affably. 'What news from London?'

'Why, Madam, none,' says he, his eyes on the ground as he made his bow.

I raised my brows. 'No?' I said. 'You come from London and can tell me no news of a marriage? What of Queen Marie, cousin?'

He drew an uneasy breath, his eyes shifting all ways, blinking nervously and turning his head as if seeking help. It came, quite innocently from Lady Clinton, who appeared with a nosegay of flowers for me, giving Norfolk the chance to bow and slink away. I let him go, for I knew what I knew.

A little later at lovely Loseley, in the gentle Surrey hills, where I was staying with Sir William More, while on Progress, Rob spoke to me of the matter. It was a beautiful day, and I was sitting carefree on cushions laid upon the doorstep into the garden, enjoying the sunshine, Rob half-kneeling beside me and one of Sir William's sons playing a lute and singing to make all delightful. Leaning his head against my knee, my hand stroking his hair, Rob said his piece.

'Norfolk fears to speak, does he?' I queried. 'He has told you this? Ay, and asked you to speak for him, I'll wager.' At this, Rob laughed and nodded. 'Is there aught 'twixt you and he, Rob?' I asked sharply. ' 'Twere better not, he is dangerous crony. Better to tell me now, see'st thou.' He disclaimed fervently and I shrugged my shoulders only half-believing. 'Well then,' I said, 'I will try him again. I cannot but give him a chance to explain; but he must tell me himself, thou knowest. I wish not to seem to accuse him.'

So at Farnham I made the opportunity. I asked Norfolk to dine alone with me, which was signal honour. He ate but little and said naught to any purpose, so after the meal, when we had risen, I gave him a sharp nip on the arm so that he winced. 'Cousin,' I said meaningly, 'I do wish you to take great heed to your pillow. What have you to say about that?'

'Your Majesty is most kind,' he mumbled, 'most kind. I thank you for the delicious meal and the graciousness of the invitation.' And that was all. He would say naught of his plans, of his writings to Marie, or of hers to him, the cow-hearted renegade.

Some days after this, we left for Basing House, the residence of old Winchester, he who had so hounded me in my young days, and whom I had forgiven, for he was useful statesman. Rob and other nobles were quartered at Titchfield House, seat of Lord Pembroke, for lack of space at Basing. While at Titchfield, Rob took sick and to his bed, sending me a message to come to his side, for he was sore distressed. I was with him at all speed and in a great worry for him, for he was a-moaning and sighing like one fit to give up his soul at any moment.

'Have you a fever, my love? Is it your head or your belly?' I asked, all agitation.

'Ah, my head!' he groaned, clutching it. 'It is in my head! Bess, it is my conscience — oh, it kills me!'

I took his hand, seating myself on the bed. 'Tell me,' I said. 'I shall understand, I promise you. Is it of Norfolk that you fret?'

And out it all came like the bursting of a boil. How he had been privy to all Norfolk's doings, his apologies for plotting against Cecil, how that Norfolk was in constant communication with Queen Marie hoping to wed her, that Rob himself had given support, half-hearted, but a certain support — oh, such regrets and misery as he was suffering, 'twas like to break his heart. He loved me, he was my man, he had behaved like a traitorous wretch, he was in a fever with it, he lamented pathetically.

'There,' I soothed, patting his hand, 'there now. Norfolk's friendship means much to you, I know. You have been a stupid fellow, have you not? Well, you have confessed and I forgive you, my dearest. But no more of such, Rob, or I shall trust you not. You have told me all you know?'

He swore that he had and, kissing him, I left him to recover while I sought out the Duke, cornering him in the Long Gallery.

'Stand, my Lord Duke!' I shouted, glaring at him fiercely. 'Now, by God's teeth, you are a dirty, whoreson knave thus to go against me! I charge you on your Oath of Allegiance to deal no further in the Scottish cause. No more lies — I know it all!'

'Nay, Majesty, nay!' he bleated, starting back like a frightened sheep. 'Nay, I have but slight regard for the Scottish Lady. Nay, I have no need to deal with her, for mine own moneys are not much less than those of all Scotland. Nay indeed, when I am in my tennis court at Norwich I feel myself, in a manner, equal with some kings. Believe me, Majesty!'

'You feel equal with kings, do you?' I snorted. 'We shall see about *that*, my Lord. 'Tis sad you behave not like one!'

After this, he left Titchfield in a hurry, returning to London, whilst I and my entourage journeyed to The Vyne, a handsome, large, red-brick mansion owned by William, Lord Sandys, where I wrote a letter to Lord Huntingdon, commanding him to take charge of Queen Marie and to curtail some of her liberties at Tutbury. It was a woundy nuisance so to be plagued when I should have been enjoying myself upon my Progress here, at The Vyne, where my father had once stayed with my mother. It spoiled all my pleasure and gave me great fret. I told Cecil to keep his ear close to the ground and discover of the doings in the North, for I feared a rebellion, and this through the work of my own kinsman! 'Twas shameful disgrace.

Returning to Windsor in September I learned the worst, and bad indeed it was. The

Earls of Northumberland and Westmorland were arming, ready to march south, Alba himself was to land at Hartlepool and Queen Marie was to be rescued from Tutbury.

'By heaven,' I said to Rob as we walked briskly along the wooden walk of the North Terrace, 'Norfolk's hand is still in this. Thou knowest that if I allow this marriage, I shall be in the Tower within four months, and she of Scotland will have my throne! Well, I shall stay here at Windsor, 'tis well fortified and see what transpires.' I kicked my heel on the boards. 'Rob, these planks are badly worn and near rotten. I must do somewhat about a new terrace when I have the time. It will not be just yet, that is for sure. Hast heard aught of Norfolk? He lies very low.'

'Ay, dearest. Cecil being busy with a letter has asked me to tell you that Norfolk has retired to Kenninghall.'

'What!' I exclaimed. 'When I have sent him not one, but several notes requesting him to Court? This is rank disobedience. Jesu, I swear he means to raise a revolt in his own country! So, then, I shall command him here, and forthwith.' I brought my foot down sharply in an irate stamp, sending it clean through the rotten wood and grazing my leg severely. The place refused to heal, giving rise to a hateful ulcerous sore that curtailed my activities greatly. I was forced to sit for long whiles with my leg up on a cushion. I bethought me, in terror, of my father's stinking, ulcerous leg, and beseeched God right heartily not to send me the same affliction. He answered my prayers kindly in the end, but not before I was constrained to go on my next Progress in a coach instead of happy and free on horse-back! 'Twas unpleasant and frightening disability.

Anyhap, my command went out to my cousin in the autumn of 1569, bringing an excuse in reply. Norfolk wrote that 'his friends were feared of his company through his Queen's displeasure, and he was feared to show himself.' He knew that he was a suspected person, the craven letter continued, and he was afraid of the Tower, 'that fortress being too great a terror for any true man.' He scribbled that he was sick, he was ill, he was near to death.

'A 'true man'!' I scoffed upon reading this effusion. 'He hath not a true bone in his body! Well, I say he *shall* come. If he is so ill he may come in a litter, but come he shall and will!' And I sent my summons swift to Kenninghall demanding his instant departure in the direction of London. At last, despite all his subterfuges and in-workings, I had him safe in the Tower, occupying rooms

37

in the Constable's lodgings, and was much relieved thereby.

Before the se'ennight was out, I had closed the ports, raised my armies and sent my Lords of Hertford and Huntingdon to stand by at Tutbury Castle, where I had ordered the Earl of Shrewsbury to double the guard on Queen Marie. Then I sent my good Lord Sussex north to command Lord Westmorland and Lord Northumberland, on their Oaths of Allegiance, to come to Court. I was in a great fret at the expense of maintaining the armies I had raised, also at the thought of their possible disloyalty if I kept them waiting with no fighting to do. This impasse was resolved on the 14th of November, for the rebel Lords captured Durham and celebrated High Mass in the cathedral there. This angered those in the South, for there were but few Catholics south of the River Trent. Thereupon I had Queen Marie moved from Tutbury to Coventry, so that when Northumberland and Westmorland arrived at nearby Selby, determined to release her, she was gone. By this time, a force, led by my dear cousin Henry Carey of Hunsdon, was also near at hand, frightening the rebels northwards once more, their armies vanishing about them as they rode. By early December, Sussex and his men faced them and they ran for the Border. Such wild and ranting rebels, and never a blow struck!

In the whole business there was but one fight, and that scarcely to the point. Norfolk's brother-in-law, the disgruntled Leonard Dacre, thwarted in his attempts to gain the Dacre inheritance, had ridden out with Sussex to quell the rising. Indeed, Sussex had commended him to me for so doing. Suddenly he seized Greystoke Castle and other Dacre properties, fortified his own castle at Naworth and called up an army of Borderers, all this after the rising was over. For sure, his chagrin and disappointment at losing to Norfolk the inheritance he considered his own had turned to whirling windmills in his head, such a grievance did he feel. 'Tis sad to see a good man turn rogue, but I could not let such goings-on continue, for the safety of my realm. So halfway through the dark, cold month of February, I sent instructions to my cousin Henry to take Dacre by force if need be. And so he did, in a resounding charge with victory in his hand. I was delighted and sent him a warm message of thanks at the end of Cecil's formal letter of congratulation. What wrote I? I can recall some of it, if I press my sad old brain as I huddle here on my pretty

39

cushions. *My Henry* . . . or some such, was it? Oh ay, now it comes:

I doubt much, my Henry, whether that the victory given me more joyed me, or that you were God-appointed the instrument of my glory; and I assure you that for my country's good, the first shall suffice, but for my heart's contentation the second more pleased me . . . . And that you may not think you have done nothing for your profit, though much for your honour, I intend to make this journey somewhat to increase your livelihood . . . Your loving kinswoman, Elizabeth R.

I writ it with mine own hand thereby to please him, the dear fellow. My hands are not now so obliging. They can scarce hold a pen for aches in the fingers. And those fingers! No longer are they as they were, exceeding long and tapering, but knotted and swollen. Why, I have had to have my precious Coronation ring sawn off, for 'twas near grown into the flesh and caused me great pain. After that I have felt never the same, for that ring was my marriage ring to England, my beloved bridegroom. Sad I feel now. Sad, heavy and melancholy. My mind is slow and inward-turned, my teeth are almost all gone, my cheeks sunken, my hair thin and snow-white under my curled, dark-red wig. Old am I, as I bite and nibble my thumb. Old, old, old, am I.

I have no heart for talk or conversation, no heart for music; I, whose life's love was music. It rings but dull and hollow on my ear. A death knell; mine own. My time here is done, I know it. Things are changing and I am too old and tired to change with them. I wish not to leave my lovely England whose heart and people are mine. I wish not to cross the dark threshold into what awaits me. Darkness and death are ahead for Elizabeth Tudor where once all was light and life. I wish not to go, but go I must, for Death's cold hand rests upon my shoulder, growing heavier by the day. But I will not rush to meet him. He must take me in my own time. I will it so, and he shall wait upon my will.

But in 1570 I was yet good to look upon. Was it not Puttenham who wrote of my bosom in such flattering terms?

Her bosom, sleek as Paris plaster,
Held up two balls of alabaster,

he wrote, lecherous rogue! I laughed over that and liked it well. Rob asked how Puttenham knew so much of my bosom and swore, in comical fashion, that he had a rival! Well, I was of an exceeding whiteness — white as Albion rocks, some said. I used but little to preserve it; a lotion of white of egg, powdered egg-shell, alum, and white poppy-seeds mixed with water that ran from under a mill-wheel. This was applied very infrequently, for I needed it but little, middle-aged though I was with thirty-seven years in my pocket.

I was fortunate in that when I came to my throne, the kind of looks I possessed were fashionable, being of the aquiline cast greatly admired, so I had no struggle to achieve the desired appearance. My time was right for me by the will of God and England. Now it is almost over, alas.

★ ★ ★

Well, we crushed the rebellion and my cousin Henry's fight was the only battle ever fought in England during the whole of my reign. The reprisals were more savage than I had intended and I am sorry for that. I wished for fines as punishments, for the most part, to cover the cost of maintaining my armies, and Cecil drafted two letters of instruction over this, although he urged for stronger measures than I wanted. Unluckily, his instructions

42

were disregarded, punishments being meted out on the spot, almost 400 miles from London, in a rage of anger, confusion and impatience by those who should have known better. Full 750 men were hanged after trial by courts-martial, in spite of Cecil's decree that civil courts be used. I thought the number hanged excessive, and liked it not at all, but the dead cannot be brought back to life, do what we will. Others were punished by deprivation and fines, clergy were unfrocked, and those who were too poor to pay or too lowly to hold slipped through the net and went free. It was a rough reckoning and, I doubt not, will be held against me as cruelty when I am gone, but desperate troubles require desperate measures, and I did wish all to understand that I was not to be trifled with.

Meanwhile, Scotland was in an uproar following the Regent Moray's death by an assassin's bullet as he rode through the streets of Linlithgow. His killer was thought to be a Hamilton, but none was ever certain o' this. 'Twas sudden end to a dark and devious man who had brought Scotland no peace despite his fair promises. In the event, he was but little worse as a ruler than his half-sister Marie whom he had forced to abdicate. A pretty crew, by my faith, but greed and pride are great levellers in the end. As it was, most of the Scots were for little King James, but Maitland of Lethington, Marie's former Secretary of State and a wily, cunning, specious fellow, put himself at the head of a party to restore his former Queen to her throne. Members of this gang constantly burst over the Border, raiding and harassing my countrymen, to my great annoyance. I sent good Sussex to deal with this, and into Scotland he went with his men, destroying all fortified places over a large mileage of southern Scotland. Yet still I could not decide whether to recognise Marie or James as Sovereign. Either course seemed to me to be fraught with difficulty, so I attended a full Council meeting on the 29th of April in order to settle my mind, if settled it could be on such a matter.

Black velvet and gold I wore, puffed with white and gold, over a jewelled kirtle. Cut very low was the bodice, to show my precious 'alabaster bosom' of Puttenham's rhyme, with a ruff and high wired collar stitched over with black and gold. I wore a dark red curled wig that day, I mind, for my hair needed washing and the days were yet chill. 'Tis better to wash the hair in summer, for then plenty of wood-ash be saved from the winter for the washing of it,

44

and drying be easy in the warm weather. A fine gold net worked with pearls I wore over the wig, and very handsome and delicate it looked.

I sat upon my armchair at the head of the table — a modern table with the top joined to elegant, stout, carven legs. Candle-sticks of silver were placed thereon, new ones of the branch socket sort, with spreading bases and grease-pans to catch the melted wax, while in the centre of the table lay some leaves of the new-fangled paper with which to blot up ink, a marvellous cunning invention. I sat upon my chair and looked down the long table at all the well-known faces turned expectantly towards me; some loved, all respected, and spoke my mind.

'My Lords,' said I, 'I will tell you that I myself am free from any determined resolution in the matter of the Scottish monarchy. I would first hear your advice and thereupon make choice of what I should think meetest for my honour.'

After a respectful pause, a very babel broke out. The old nobility and my Rob wished for the restoration of Marie, while Cecil, Bacon and Sir Walter Mildmay favoured the little King's party. We argued back and forth so vigorously that at last Nick Bacon, ever choleric, roared that he would count himself out of Council if I recognised not good advice when it was in my ears. At this I laughed and beat upon the table for quiet.

'See now,' quoth I, 'I will draw up a set of terms for Queen Marie. Ay, strong terms, my Lords, fear not, and she must accept them. You and I, my Cecil, will draft this up, and with it you will visit the Queen to secure her agreement. She will agree for she is in no position to do otherwise. And while this goes forward, I will keep King James's party in funds — therefore quiet — so all will run easy for the nonce.'

None was best pleased at this, of course, for it smacked too much of compromise, but I intended to keep the matter under mine own hand to manage as I wished. Hey, it was the devil of a year! I felt I needed six heads and an hundred eyes in each to keep pace with events, but I succeeded well enough with what God had given me. Ay, and I was excommunicated too. There was a thing! It set all by the ears.

Upon the 25th of May 1570, Corpus Christi Day, a Papal Bull was found affixed to the door of the house in Paul's Churchyard of John Aylmer, Bishop of London. Pope Pius V, who had issued it, was a fool, his head in the clouds, his wits a century behind the

46

times. He had put out the Bull without a word to France nor Spain and nearly caused an international incident through the consequent misunderstandings it brought. None of my government knew of it, in spite of its having been published three months earlier. I was enraged, for it inferred that the Papacy had never recognised my Sovereignty. This was all untrue, for the two Popes before that stupid old noddy-head had recognised me as Queen without question.

'God Almighty!' I shouted to Cecil when we heard of it. ' 'Tis bad enough that my secret service sleeps, but it seems we have traitors under our noses! Who is he that put up the thing? He shall suffer for it, I promise you! Dost realise that if my Catholics now wish to be loyal to me they disobey the Pope, and if they are loyal to him they are disloyal to me? 'Tis exactly what I have wished to avoid! Oh, it makes me burn, Cecil — and so shall the dog who posted that Bull!'

'Execution would be better,' he murmured, pursing his lips. 'We want no reminders of your sister's fiery punishments, do we?'

'Ha, you are right,' I exclaimed. 'Well, I leave it to you then. Let it be a warning to all who would disaffect, say I.'

So John Fenton, who had posted the Papal Bull, came to his death, being executed.

Ambassador de Spes chose to be appalled at such *grandissimo crueldad*, as he wrote in a despatch, the contents of which were secretly copied for me to read. So dainty as the Spanish were growing, my oath! 'Twas not so long since the Inquisition when many ghastly atrocities were practised, and all in the name of God, too, such hypocrites as they were! Besides, Fenton's death was the usual kind for a traitor — 'twas nothing extraordinary. We are the children of our times, after all.

As it was, I gave Fenton's widow a dispensation to hear Mass in her own house for the rest of her life. Her man was but doing what he considered to be his duty, and had told Lord Sussex upon the scaffold that he wished me no harm. He even gave Sussex a diamond ring worth £400 to give to me, poor gentleman. 'Twas sad thing, but a ruler must be above sentiment — 'tis horrid truth as I discovered soon enough in my reigning.

In full summer I felt that I might try myself as bed-bait again. I sent a messenger to the Archduke Charles of Austria, my erstwhile ardent suitor, for England had no allies and Austria might be useful. However, a slap in the face awaited me here, for although still single, he was also too wary of me to be caught this time, and wed himself off, fast, to a Catholic Princess, to end as a persecutor of Protestants. I could not, in honesty, blame him. He had done his best, in years past, to agree to my every whim in order to win me who would not be won, so I took his disaffection in good part, turning my eyes elsewhere. I turned them to France, for while there was no love lost between our two countries, the Dowager Queen Catherine de' Medici had three sons. The King, her eldest, also my former suitor, had since wed, but her second Prince, the Duke of Anjou, was at liberty. I decided to consider him.

Admitted, he had nineteen years to my thirty-seven, but a crown covers much, and the Dowager Queen coveted a throne for each of her boys. Also, an alliance with England was attractive to her, for France was feared that England would befriend Spain, while Spain was equally feared that England would ally with France. Thus, laughing up my sleeve, I began negotiations. We would see whither they led. I sent a new and clever young gent called Francis Walsingham to deal with the affair. He had been well recommended by Cecil as having a real feeling for secret service work, a man after his own heart, he said. A handsome man was this Walsingham, and known to me through my

49

cousins the Careys, while being own brother-in-law to Sir Walter Mildmay, my Chancellor of the Exchequer. Ever had I a fancy for dark, aquiline men, and Walsingham was as dark as any Moor. That became my little name for him in later years. My Moor, I called him.

★ ★ ★

I had allowed Norfolk to leave the Tower and dwell in his own palace in the Charterhouse, under house-arrest, for he was kin to me and of great rank. I wished him to have another chance to redeem himself if he would. But all through the autumn he was treasonous. The spies I had posted in his household informed me of this, but could get no proof from his own hand, for he would put naught of his messages to Queen Marie and Roberto di Ridolfi in writing. So we had to wait, for proof would surely show itself in the end.

It was during this year of 1570 that the bells were first heard on the 17th of November to mark the day of my ascension to the throne of England twelve years before. I was touched to tears by the charm and sweetness of such a gesture of love when so many seemed to be against me. This gesture has been repeated every year since, on Ascension Day, when England's bells ring in thanks and devotion to me, Queen of the fairest isle in all the world. Ah, handsome and lively was I then. Now — well, better I turn my poor old mind back to those days, the days of my perfidious kinsman, coward and traitor as he was.

What a fool, with such a weak headpiece, to go in for such strong business! He should have left it alone, for in less than eight months the matter was revealed when Charles Bailly, a Catholic agent, was taken and searched at Dover. In his baggage were discovered letters for Queen Marie's go-between, the Bishop of Ross, touching the Duke and his plans. A pretty budget, indeed!

Bailly betrayed the Bishop when racked, and disclosed the cipher they had used. Straightway, Ross was taken and placed under the charge of the Bishop of Ely at Ely Place in Holborn. So we awaited events and they were not long in forthcoming.

I had created my cherished William Cecil Baron of Burghley earlier that year. He more than merited it, and I wished him to have a good standing with the Lords in Parliament, for it was necessary to call for funds, the Treasury having grown dangerously low. This measure worked well, and the Lords, under Cecil's guidance, disappointed me not. 'Twas

51

very different with the wretched Commons, who suddenly raised a point that would, if taken notice of, have debarred both Queen Marie and her son from the Succession.

'God's wounds!' I railed to Cecil. 'Have they no sense in their thick heads? I wish *nothing* to be done about the Succession, thou knowest. I saw what happened when my sister Mary lay a-dying in London, when all left her side to take the road for Hatfield and me, and she in agony of body and mind, poor thing. I tell you, I was sickened and I vowed then, that never should it happen to me. If I name a successor, plots will arise. If those two are debarred, plots will arise. I wish the matter left alone. These Commons have shown themselves right audacious, arrogant and presumptuous. How dare they attempt to make such a Bill? The new Treasons Bill is bad enough, allowing far too much governmental interference over the handling of traitors, without dragging in Marie and James. No, I will not have it!' I said decisively, slamming my hand upon the table so that the new Lord Burghley fairly started back. 'I mislike this new Bill very much, being not of the mind to offer extremity or injury to any person. I will have it re-drafted to my satisfaction.'

And so I did, speaking firmly to the

Commons, ending in amity with a compromise, as was ever my way. I had been forced to shut my heart over the matter of John Fenton and I liked not that matter. I would not have too much killing and cruelty without my let.

Through all this tergiversation I had missed my springtime hunting at Nonsuch, that beautiful palace built by my father for his delight and the astonishment of all who beheld it. It lies within a lovely park, one side of which is skirted by the lane to the little market town of Epsham. Upon a sunny day Nonsuch flashes like a box of jewels, for set in its turreted façades are a myriad pieces of coloured glass of all shapes and sizes, placed to catch the light; a wondrous fancy and vastly pleasing to the eye. By moonlight it is a fairy dream. Indeed, I have never seen aught like it, and it is rightly named, for in sooth, there is none such.

In the garden there is a fine tricksy fountain made like a pyramid all of marble, but full of pipes which may spit upon all who come within reach unaware. 'Twas amazing how the unpopular Spanish Ambassador de Spes was constantly given a wetting, while all around were quite unable to stay their mirth, laughing near to piss themselves. My God, it was right comical! There is such a fountain at Hampton too. A splendid high

53

and massy structure, it stands in the first court, and will suddenly give those nearby a soaking, all of us crowing almost to die with the joke. Well do I remember our gaiety round those whimsical waterworks. I could almost laugh now at the memory, had I the lightness of heart to do so, but all is now heaviness with me, I fear . . .

Because of further revelations in the wretched plottings of Norfolk, Cecil urged me not to go on Progress, but I scouted the idea.

'Nay, my Lord!' I cried. 'Be not so afeared for my safety. We have the plot well in hand, and I would not miss my Progress for a ransom. 'Tis all arranged, and how I do wish to go! I shall be a-horseback this time, and not in a bumpy coach as I was last year by reason of the damned sore on my leg. Thank God 'tis now healed! The journeying will be a welcome rest and change for me. Besides, if I am in Essex, 'tis my guess that the rest of East Anglia will prove doubly loyal after the Duke of Norfolk's defection.'

And off I went, first to Hampton Court, then to Hatfield where I stayed for several weeks reliving old memories and revisiting old haunts. I stayed at Audley End, too, for a few days, after which I and my train made our way to Thaxted and Horham Hall, a fine moated mansion lying a mile down the lane from the town. This house had been begun in Henry VII, my grandsire's reign, by old John Cutte. Cutte's grandson, also John, was a very Croesus of wealth who delighted in showing his hospitality, so I decided he could show me some of it. Jesu, the man must have been a Midas! Many of my nobles could not have outshone him, a mere baronet. There was a tower built especial for me to watch the hunting and to shoot from also, every window of the house being full of coloured glass, there was wall-panelling of the best, a floor of marble — eh, 'twas splendid. So pleased and impressed was I that I remained there a full nine days. Cecil and I had many a talk in the sumptuous Withdrawing Room assigned to me, and drafted there several letters concerning Norfolk and Queen Marie.

In fact, 'twas while I was at Horham that the plot broke, for a certain draper called Thomas Browne, being asked to carry a bag of £50 in money from the Charterhouse to a point where he would deliver it to someone else, grew suspicious. The bag was too heavy for what it should have contained and the good fellow broke it open, discovering therein 300 golden French crowns, 300 English angels, and letters in cipher to Marie's adherents in Scotland. Horrified, he reported his find at once and a search of the Charterhouse took place immediately. Soon enough, there was found, under a mat near a window, a letter in cipher from Marie herself, thus confirming all surmises.

At once Cecil left Horham in great haste for London, and in the midst of night, had Norfolk escorted straight back to the Tower. The next morning, after a minute search, Cecil found the translation of the cipher letters in Browne's bag. This was writ on papers hid behind some tiles, and with it, he was able to decipher the letters and discover that they implicated Norfolk directly in the plot. More letters and more ciphers were found in his books; one code being found even under a tile on the roof! The place was a very nest of treachery. Indeed, I was glad to be at Horham and away from London and such goingson. I have seldom stayed anywhere in such comfort save in mine own palaces, offering to return again to Horham one day. Instead of looking alarmed at the prospect of such cost to him, good Cutte beamed his pleasure.

'I will look forward to it, Madam,' he said. 'I count it as a promise. Remember!' he cried, as I and my train trotted out of the gate, 'Remember, Majesty, you are to come again!'

'I will, Sir Croesus!' I called back in answer. 'I have been too well entertained not to do so!'

And I kept my word, returning some years later.

* * *

Once back at Richmond, I fell suddenly ill with the old wambling gut-gripes and a violent migraine that knocked me to my bed as one felled by a blow. I scarce knew what I was about, so deathly sick did I feel. After a day or two I was mercifully relieved by attacks of severe vomiting which left me weak but restored, more or less, to myself.

I lay on my daybed in the oriel window overlooking the sweet waters of the Thames and the quiet green banks of Twittenham Park on the Middlesex side. I had my cousin Kate Carey with me — she who had wed the son of my good old uncle Lord William Howard of Effingham — and pretty Lenna von Snakenburg too. They were working at chair-covers for Loseley Park, for I had promised some to Sir William More. We had been busy a-stitching at them for nigh on a twelvemonth and were near done

57

with the fiddling things.

'Jesu,' I sighed, 'but my fingers are too weak to hold a needle. Why should my damned belly play me these tricks? I have eaten naught to throw it to such seizures, God knows.'

'Your Majesty has been much fretted,' suggested Helena in her charming Swedish-English, 'and when you fret, this is the result, no?'

'Ay indeed,' agreed Kate. ' 'Tis always the same, dear Madam. You know it is so. So much have you been put about by the perfidy of His Grace of Norfolk that I think it a wonder you have held up so long. Cecil — I mean Lord Burghley — was desperate anxious about you. I'll swear he saw death hanging over you, ready to strike at any moment. I heard him tell Sir Nicholas Bacon that all knew that the safety of this realm rests upon your health.'

'Oh me, is he at that again?' I smiled at the two sweet, earnest faces turned so concernedly towards me. 'If I worry, so does he. More, I should guess. He is always imagining England without me, seeing chaos in my very shadow. Nay, I do not mean to die yet, my dears. I have too much to do to spare the time in dying!'

They laughed and our talk turned to other

58

matters. I recovered swift enough and was as well as ever, to Cecil's relief. Well enough to set in hand the building of a stone terrace at Windsor to replace the old wooden way along the northern side. 'Twas more than time it was done. I needed somewhere to take my morning walk there, now that my leg was healed, Jesu be praised.

I was well enough, also, to encourage an exceeding handsome gent at my Court. He was not new there, having come first to my attention ten years before, when I had seen him dancing as Master of the Game at the Inner Temple one Christmastide. I liked men, enjoyed their stimulating presence about me, took pleasure in the sight, smell and sound of them. I loved to raise the flames of desire in them too, for I was very woman, though crippled in the heart through what I had seen and known in my childhood. Flirtation eased my mind from cares of state, made me feel as if I had more of blood and less of ink and policies in my veins, and this man, of a sudden, made my blood beat quite fast. He was not just a handsome face and a shapely body, neither. Nay, Sir Christopher Hatton, who was now a Member of Parliament for Higham Ferrers, had loyalty, honesty and brains. I had had ten years to assess these qualities and found them well to my taste, as well as his outstanding good looks. I began to favour him and found him charming, with the tact and good temper of an angel, the dear creature. His religious views matched with mine too, and we had many an interesting talk, I discovering that he was an excellent speaker and well-informed, with a great love of music. His dancing was even more sprightly and delightful than when I had first noticed him, and he began to rival Rob as my most favoured partner in that joyous exercise.

Oh, how I did love to step it! I would dance six or seven galliards of a morning, after being dressed, for sheer joy of prancing to music. It enlivened all my body and raised my senses in the most charming fashion, and oft did Sir Kit partner me morning and evening. Rob was not best pleased at this and showed me a sullen face, but oh, I needed somewhat to take my thoughts from the heavy business of poor, foolish Norfolk whose future was dark indeed. He would be sentenced to death, no doubt of it, and the warrant would be brought for me to sign. I shied away from that idea quick as a startled mare. I would deal with that when the time should come. Meanwhile, I meant to bask in the increasingly ardent gaze of beautiful Sir

Kit who was rapidly falling deep in love with me. I gave him many gratuities too, for love is precious gift and should be rewarded.

* * *

I could not, for long, avoid the matter of Norfolk, for in the month of January he was brought to his trial, found guilty and sentenced to death by disembowelling, quartering and the like. Well, I would not have that. He was of next rank to mine own, and if he came to his death at all 'twould be by the axe as befitted his station. Four times the amended sentence was brought to me, but each time my heart fainted and I could not sign it, havering about until March when I fell very ill. 'Twas my wretched belly again, but no migraine this time. Nay, I had eaten of tainted fish and nigh met my death through it.

Lord Burghley, as I must call my Cecil now, and dearest Rob spent three days and nights at my bedside, in true fear for my life, before my fever abated somewhat, leaving me weak as a mawworm. I could transact no business and Parliament was called to deal with affairs. This took matters out of my hands, for the Commons and Peers shouted for the death of Queen Marie as well as Norfolk. Sick though I was, I resisted this with all the force that was in me to command, but it became apparent that to save Marie, Norfolk must be sacrificed. I felt it to be a sacrifice, moreover, for Norfolk though a fool and a treacherous one, was near kin to me and had been high in my regard. But Marie, no matter what she was as a person, was a Sovereign and under my hand. I could not have her killed for these very reasons.

I faced my Council bravely, and God's feet, they were all glaring at me grim enough. 'Nay!' I cried. 'Can I put to death the bird that to escape the hawk, has fled to my feet for protection? Honour and conscience forbid!'

I heard exasperated sighs, saw mouths twist and eyes turn up, but I stood firm. Yet, although I might save Marie, in the case of Norfolk there was no escape for him or for me. Every one of my Protestants was against me all over the realm. There was naught for it — I had to bow to the inevitable and sign the warrant. In all my reign there had been no noble put to death by beheading, and the scaffold on Tower Hill had fallen to bits after fourteen years without custom. It was necessary to build another, therefore, and I found this a very painful reflection.

Norfolk seemed to recover his senses at the last, behaving with great courage and dignity, I heard, dying on the morn of the 2nd of June at one chop of the axe, very quiet and brave. I was right upset about it all from start to finish. I felt his blood to be on Marie's head; yet another man had died through her machinations. 'Twas at this time I writ a piece of poesie, for the thing was much in my mind.

> ... For falsehood now doth flow, I
>   wrote, and subject's faith doth ebb,
> Which would not be if Reason ruled, or
>   Wisdom weaved the web ...
> The Daughter of Debate, that eke
>   discord doth sow,
> Shall reap no gain where former rule
>   hath taught still Peace to grow.

There was more of it, but it irks my old mind to attempt to recall it. The Daughter of Debate indeed she was and discord did she bring to my England and me.

2

YEARS OF PROGRESS
1572 – 1578

We lost the ancient and venerable Marquis of Winchester in death during that spring of 1572. Although he had been cruel to me in my youth, he had served me faithfully and well since I had become Queen, and I had made him my Lord High Treasurer. In spite of his thin and wizened appearance, he had lived to be eighty-seven years old and had 103 grandchildren, a rare blessing of God.

I gave his post to my invaluable Burghley, thus leaving the State Secretaryship vacant. Straightway I decided upon Francis Walsingham and Tom Smith to fill this, jointly. They were excellent statesmen, both cunning, secret, and loyal to me. I had need of such, and in such God never denied me.

In the same spring was settled the Treaty of Blois, under which England and France became allies, so that England was no longer isolated, and any French interference in the matter of Marie of Scots was at an end. It was a great relief to me and my government.

Very shortly after this, while I was at Oatlands, finally recovering from my illness by hunting and refreshing myself in the quiet and sweet airs, Burghley came to me with a message. I was in my private cabinet playing backgammon with my cousin Kate before the time of dining, when he bowed himself into the room, a letter in his hand.

'Ha, from France, I'll wager,' I said, setting down the silver dicebox and motioning Kate to stay. 'The Duke of Anjou makes difficulties?'

'Ay, Madam, Walsingham and Smith write that he insists upon being allowed full Catholic Mass with all rites and panoplies if he weds you.'

'The devil he does! Sit ye my Lord, your gout troubles you I can see. Come, what more?'

Seating himself with a grunt upon a cushion-topped chest, Burghley told me that in case of my refusing the arrogant Anjou, his younger brother, the Duke of Alençon, had been put forward for my consideration. 'He is no beauty,' remarked Burghley dubiously.

'So I have heard,' I replied. 'Short and pock-marked, was what I heard. Very short and very pock-marked. Scarcely an Adonis, besides being but seventeen years old.'

'Well,' said Burghley, making the best of

65

it, ' 'tis said that the pock marks are no great disfigurement because they are thick rather than deep or great. Those upon the blunt end of his nose *are* great and deep, but how much misliked may as it please God to move the beholder.'

'I have no intention of beholding him or his pock marks yet,' I said. 'How tall is this pocky youth, Sir Spirit?'

'He is the same size as myself, and I am no dwarf.'

I gave a derisive snort. 'Say rather the height of your grandson!'

'He is but seventeen, he may grow. And his beard will certainly grow,' he added. 'That will serve to cover many of the pock marks.'

'A second Kit Hatton, no less!' laughed wickedly. At this, Kate giggled aloud and even Burghley permitted himself an austere smirk.

'Anyhap,' went on Burghley, 'he is afire for the match, saying that his affection for your Majesty is unfeigned and great.'

'Well, he may write to me and we shall see,' I said.

I doubted the sincerity of the little Frenchman, for he had never seen me, but 'twas amusing nonetheless. At worst, he was not insolent like his brother who had called me 'an old woman with a sore leg'! I meant to pursue the match for as long as was convenient; 'twould keep France sweet and a willing ally. Besides, I liked courtship, had grown used to it; it was delightful to be sought after, and although Rob and I were still close, much of the fire and ardency had gone from our relationship. He was a hot-blooded creature, needing women to bed with. Jealous though I am, and greedy of love, yet I am not devoid of understanding. Nay, I knew Rob would have his adventures, and so long as they were not obvious to me, I was fairly content to wink an eye — indeed to close both on occasion. So long as he remained at Court, devoted-seeming by my side, I was pleased to be pleased. After all, I had Kit Hatton sighing passionately over me, ardent letters from my impetuous little, pocky Frenchman, and a new young man was entreating my smiles also.

This put Kit into a taking, for he grew desperate jealous of this new young man. Edward de Vere, Earl of Oxford he was, idol of my Maids of Honour and but recently wed to Burghley's daughter Ann. That was an unfortunate business, for although Oxford had been a royal ward, brought up in Burghley's house since the age of twelve, he was handsome as to person but not as to nature. When he had asked for Ann Cecil she was wild for him, and though Burghley did his best to dissuade her, in the end he could not deny her. Well, upon the surface, it was a good match. Unhappy little soul, she was but fifteen at the time of the marriage and no beauty. 'Twas the money that came with her he wanted, and the influence of Burghley as father-in-law to save his cousin of Norfolk, which Burghley did not use, thus earning Oxford's enmity. He led Ann a wretched life, treating her badly and slandering her most cruelly, and there was naught could be done about it. Once wed, the woman is her husband's property as is her fortune. 'Tis life. My poor Spirit had taken a real cuckoo into his happy nest in the shape of the young Earl of Oxford.

I found him dazzlingly attractive at first, so handsome, gallant and witty, full of outrageous sayings, and he fluttered round me like a moth round a candle flame, but I tired of him in time, for he had no ballast, no weight, and a plaguey unstable disposition. He would not do for any important post at Court or abroad, and while I like my men to be well-looking, they must also be trustworthy and of use to me. I wish no useless butterflies about me, nay, not even now, when I am nothing but an ugly old bone-bag. To ease my poor Kit's torments I made him Captain of the Gentleman Pensioners, which was signal favour among the many I gave him. Dear fellow, he was not dashing like Rob, nor audacious like Oxford, but big, gentle and nobly-beautiful. Such soft, dark eyes, such a tender, expressive mouth, yet strong and manly withal. It did me good but to gaze upon him, but no matter how oft I whispered this to him, the thought of Oxford's presence acted like gall upon him, fretting his kind heart sadly. It was 'long of me that he never wed, for none other than his Queen would do for handsome Kit Hatton, so he took no other to wife. 'Tis not many women can boast of that, especially when there were dozens who would have been glad and happy to take second place in his heart. It was balm to my restless spirit.

I had a delightful Progress that summer. The weather was pleasant, so travelling was not too irksome, and those who had to dwell in tents, there being no other lodging for them, moaned and groaned not so loudly as usual. And for those who did groan, I noted that they did not stay away! We took our way through Hertfordshire and Bedfordshire, staying at great houses on the way, until we came to Warwick Castle. To this I had much looked forward, for my cherished Ann, wife to Rob's brother Ambrose the Earl of Warwick, was to entertain me there. Ah, that castle is a lovely place, so beautifully set by the Avon which runs down in cascades, the sweet rushing of the waters being plainly heard in all the best rooms. My three hundred careware baggage carts were soon unpacked, horses were stabled, lodgings were found, tents were set up — all ran as smooth as oil — for dear Ann knew well what was expected, having accompanied me in her place as young Maid-of-Honour in the years before her marriage to Ambrose.

There was a dance of rustic men and maidens held in the courtyard while I was there; 'twas delightful, for all were so merry and the music so insistent that I clapped my hands to keep the time, and all my Court imitated me throughout the dances with much cheering and laughter. The Earl Ambrose and his sweet lady also arranged a wondrous display of fireworks and crackers for me, causing sighs and exclamations of amazement at the explosions, flames and showers of sparks. It was right cleverly done and all were entertained until the sighs changed to screams and shrieks.

A spark had lodged in the thatch of a nearby cottage, burning the entire roof clean off. It could have been dire tragedy, but none were hurt, thanks be to God. I was greatly upset, sending my people to find the poor owners and having them brought, all wet, grimed and sobbing before me, when I told them to be of good cheer. I and my folks would give them money for another roof, I said, for I had been told that the building itself was safe. We swiftly collected £25.13.8 which was well in excess of the amount needed, and well-deserved too for their dismay and trouble. I bade Ambrose and Ann give them lodging until the roof was mended, which they were pleased to do. The man, Henry Cooper, fell on his knees to me.

'Majesty, 'tis too much — we can get a new roof for less. Will ye not take some back?'

'Nay, honest Cooper,' quoth I, 'keep all. 'Tis for your trouble. I would not have any of my English men distressed 'long of me.'

Whilst at Warwick, I rode over to my Rob's great house at Kenilworth in Leicestershire, taking but a few attendants, to spend two days in private with him, very fond and loving. Then back to Warwick for a while, and after that, officially to Kenilworth in state.

I was out riding with Rob, jumping and racing in the park, when despatches were brought to me. I could see 'twas of grave import, so read them at once, whilst on horseback, and learned the first news of the ghastly massacre of 4,000 Huguenots and their noble leaders in Paris, and as many elsewhere in France, upon the 24th of August, St. Bartholomew's Day. Calling to Rob, I galloped straightway back to the house, summoning Burghley at once to my side. The French Ambassador, de la Mothe Fénélon, who was in my train, I would not have near me. He wished to explain — to explain! As if such could ever be satisfactorily explained! My country would be enraged, my ministers were horrified, my clerics aghast. Indeed, Aylmer, Bishop of London, besought Burghley to have Queen Marie executed at once, before any trouble could be caused here. But I temporised. We were due to leave Kenilworth for Woodstock, and during that time I formulated my plans, although not without heated discussions upon the way.

Once at Woodstock — ah, here was a place of memories! 'Twas in this palace that I lived, a poor prisoner, during my sister Mary's troubled reign. Then the place had been nigh ruinous, but since my accession I had seen to it that it had been restored and maintained as was fitting for a royal palace. It was right comfortable, and I smiled to myself, thinking of the contrast 'twixt then and now. Yet I could do little of smiling, for the news from France shocked and sickened us all. I spoke seriously to my Council of it.

'I have decided to interview Fénélon,' I said. 'It will not be easy, but it must be done.' They burst into frenzied arguments and differing modes of advice. Holding up my hand for silence, I went on: 'Now, hark ye. I do not wish to upset our alliance with France, my Lords. Nor do I wish to seem to condone such terrible doings in any way. But we must not lose our senses over this. Nay, Rob,' I said, as he made to protest, black eyes flashing indignantly, 'think a little, hot-head. If we fall out with France, the way is open for Spain and France together to war upon us. We should have no hope of survival. Later perhaps, but not now, my dear.'

'What do you suggest, Bess, my love?' he asked, exchanging fiery glances with Kit who had accompanied me, and who showed annoyance at Rob's intimate use of my name.

'I think we should behave quiet, dignified and quelling,' said I. 'Dear Burghley, what sayest thou that we should dress all in black as a sign of mourning, to greet Fénélon, and all remain silent as a token of respect to those so foully slain?'

'I think it well, Madam,' he admitted, ' 'Twill be impressive without laying ourselves open to charges of actual accusation.'

'See to it then, my Spirit,' I charged him, and so 'twas done.

On the 8th of September I received Fénélon in state. The hapless Ambassador had to pass through several ante-rooms where black-clad courtiers waited in silence, staring at the ground. At last he came to the Presence Chamber, where I stood with my chief ladies and my Privy Councillors in a semicircle, all in black. Poor Fénélon looked ready to faint away. Advancing to meet him, cold and stern, I took him aside to a window embrasure.

'And what have you to say, my Lord?' I asked him, quiet and grave.

Fénélon stammered, in French, that an attempt to murder the French King had been discovered, and that justice had demanded strong reprisals. No enmity had been intended against the Protestant Powers, he faltered, his heart clearly not in this lame explanation.

'Dost think that justice did demand the murder of so many women and children?' I queried. 'I fear that those who led your King to abandon his natural subjects might lead him to abandon his alliance with me.'

At last I withdrew and left him to my Councillors who swinged him roundly. I heard that Burghley cried that the massacre was the greatest crime since the Crucifixion. It was, indeed, a disgrace to France. I felt it very much, so much that when one of my secretaries wrote, in a note to France, a flattering reference to two Queens both so experienced in arts of government, I flew into a rage and ordered the words stricken out.

'Take heed what you write for me, sirrah!' I cried. '*My* arts of government are very different from those employed by the Queen Mother of France!'

★ ★ ★

There was still great pressure upon me for the death of Queen Marie. I could not but agree that it would be better were she not upon this earth at all. For all that, it was impossible for me to assent to an official killing by an English Parliamentary decree — 'twould bring all the might of Spain down upon me and serve to arouse the French Catholics again. I had saved Marie from her own people once, and precious little good it had brought me; merely the treachery of the head of the English nobility in the shape of Norfolk, while behind him, Marie had done her best to activate the plot to murder me. I regretted having rescued her from her countrymen. Mayhap mine honour and conscience had been a little too sensitive on that point, I reflected. I told Burghley so and I told Rob so. At last we called Sir Harry Killigrew to a private meeting, the four of us only, and instructed him to go to Scotland and turn the conversation so that Lord Mar, the new Regent, would of himself, ask for Marie to be given up to the Scots for execution.

'See you, Sir Harry,' said Burghley quietly, 'you must agree to Mar's proposal, should he make it, but only on the condition that Queen Marie's head be off within four hours. Speed is essential in this affair, and secrecy too.'

'Ay,' I broke in, but softly, 'for if aught leaks out, you will die for it, Sir Harry. 'Tis dangerous mission, for you could die for it at our hands, we being unable to condone such doings openly.'

The doughty Sir Harry, ever daring, left for Scotland and found Lord Mar willing, but wanting so much coin in exchange that the whole business smacked of blackmail. Burghley said that Sir Harry should not even have listened to such greedy proposals, while I was beginning to feel anxious about the whole affair, wishing I had never let it go forward, as I confided to Rob soon after at Windsor.

'I would we had never begun it!' I cried distractedly. 'I refuse to abide by Mar's terms. God's death, but Marie might be dead already by secret means of the Regent. I wish to stop the affair, Rob, for God's sake I do!' And I burst into tears. He attempted to soothe me with kisses and caresses, saying that all could be safely left to Burghley, but I started up again at that. 'Burghley *wants* her dead!' I sobbed. 'He does not feel about her as do! I feel two ways about her — thou knowest it!'

At last he got me to lie upon my bed and sleep, as I usually did in the evenings, for although I was often early abroad with the sun, 'twas mostly because I had not gone to bed of a night. I was not a morning woman, see'st thou, and did much work during the night hours, having been poor at sleep since a youngling. I would take naps during the day if I felt weary, as well as my accustomed evening one. When I woke from my repose, a letter had come from Burghley at Westminster to say that the Earl of Mar had suddenly died. At this I went into an hysterical fit, raving and wailing, feeling sure that all was in train for an underhand murder of Marie before any could stay it. Again Rob soothed me, giving soft reasons to my ladies for my state of agitation, but, sensible fellow, he apprised Walsingham of the facts and wrote to Burghley to come to Windsor.

Sweet Rob, since Norfolk's death he was changed. He had made a friend of Walsingham, was trusted by Burghley and was my support and comfort as no other. Little did I know that he was leading two lives! Little did I know that he and the daughter of my great-uncle Lord Howard of Effingham were at bed-sport — nay had been so for nigh on a year! My dear uncle, who as Lord William Howard, had stood my protector in my young days of terror, had two lovely daughters, Douglas and Frances, who were ladies of my Court. Douglas was wed to Lord Sheffield, but I knew she had a great fancy for Rob, as had her sister, indeed as had many of the Court ladies. That was nothing strange, although I did think the two girls inclined to act more than usual foolish over him and reprimanded them for their behaviour.

When Lord Sheffield died of a sudden, my Rob, all secret, troth-plighted Douglas at a house in Cannon Row, Westminster. Why, in the same year that her father, my beloved uncle died, she bore Rob a son! And he promised to wed her. If I had known!

God's nails, 'twere best I did not, for I should have wanted to kill them both. That little Douglas Sheffield should have known the secrets of my darling Rob's body and borne him a son — why, it would have sent me crazed. So I found it out later, as did everyone else; the child could not be hid for ever, such a beautiful boy — and my heart and belly were wrung with anguish. But that came later . . .

* * *

Ay, my dear uncle Lord William, Baron Howard of Effingham, breathed his last in the bleak, grey days of January. Uncle to my mother, he had ever a kindness for me and stood firm 'twixt me and death a-many times when I was young and hunted like a helpless beast by mine enemies. He died at his house in Reigate and was buried in the church there, for Reigate was in his demesne. I would have made him Earl had he possessed enough funds, but he was always a lavish spender, having bought the lands in Surrey to add to those he owned by royal grant. Unfortunately, one must have sufficient monies to support a rise in rank. He was annoyed with me over it, the old fire-eater, and called me a penny-pincher in a voice to lift the roof. I hoped he might lean towards my saving ways, but he was too old to change. We made up our quarrel, but when I heard of his Will I was forced to laugh, albeit ruefully. He had begun the document with a bequest to me and left it blank! Ah, he was never one to mince his words, the fine old gentleman — after all, I did possess more than he, and he had a family — but I felt the rebuke nonetheless. He had the last word there, that was sure.

My cherished Kit fell desperate ill in May with an affliction of the kidneys and I was frantic with worry, visiting his bedside every day. Rob and I fell out over it, 'twas natural enough.

'So, you have finished your sick-nursing today,' he remarked acidly as we sat in a pleached arbour at Windsor, the sun flickering through the leaves and dappling my peach-coloured satin skirts and his blue and crimson doublet with moving shadows. 'I wonder you have time for me.'

'Now Rob, be not tiresome,' I protested. 'Sir Kit is sick almost to die.'

'I wish he would then,' grumbled my disgruntled lover. 'For my part, could he breathe his last this instant I should be delighted. It seems that I touch your cold heart no longer and you care not for my sorrow. Hatton has all your intent, and I, after all these years, am nothing. Well, Madam, you may love me no more, but there are others who do!' he finished defiantly.

My lips tightened. 'Indeed!' I said sharply. 'No doubt you mean The Ladies Frances Howard and Douglas Sheffield who are making themselves laughing-stocks over you. Well, neither shall have you, so you may forget it. You but try to make me as jealous as yourself.'

He said no more, but turned the subject with singular adroitness, although his olive cheek had flushed slightly. Ah, if I had known! If I had known! That sly Sheffield cat had his child even then and had gone through some sort of mock-marriage with him. To shut her mouth, no doubt.

Rob was pleased enough when I sent Kit off to Spa in the Low Countries, in the care of mine own good Dr. Julio, to take the cure. I missed Kit's sweet presence greatly and was not comforted by Rob's cock-lofty behaviour in his absence. He wrote me some beautiful letters while he was away. I joyed in them, for here was his heart upon paper.

. . . *Would God I were with you but for one hour,* he wrote. *My wits are overwrought with thoughts. I find myself amazed. Bear with me, my most dear, sweet Lady. Passion overcometh me. I can write no more. Love me; for I love you . . .* And he signed it *Your poor Lids,* for that was my little name for him, writing Δ Δ to signify Eyelids.

I knew well that he loved me. Passion frequently overcame him when we were alone together. He was right hot-blooded, see'st thou, and his flame warmed my cool not a little. His delightful letters followed me all through Kent when I went there on Progress. I had one at Sandwich, where I stayed for four days with Mr. and Mrs. Manwoode, and another one at Cranbrooke, the famous weaving town, a populous, rich, busy place with fine modern houses.

Ha, I recall 'twas at Cranbrooke that they laid the broadcloth down for me. I was to visit with Walter Henle of Coursehorn, and a length of grey broadcloth was laid down a goodly stretch along the way, a pretty fancy which pleased me well. Early in the day I had alighted from my horse at the George Inn, a handsome house with a fine staircase, and received a deputation of townsmen in the Court Room up the stair. They gave me a goodly cup, I mind, of silver-gilt, fine decorated and enamelled. Yea . . . Then I walked part of the way to Coursehorn along the cloth, while all the folk cheered and called my name, before re-mounting and trotting off to the manor house. I could not tarry long, for I was expected at Hemsted that even. I had enjoyed Cranbrooke, finding it a charming, pretty town, and delighting in my visit there. Indeed, I granted a charter to the school the year after. Yea . . . I mind it . . . so long ago . . .

Rob and I were forty that year of 1573. What a mort o' years! I scrutinised his handsome face oft enough for marks of age upon it, but saw mighty few. I scrutinised mine own also. In all honesty, I looked not near my years. My countenance bore no lines, my jaw sagged not, nor did my neck, that tell-tale spot. Sometimes my eyes showed a little puffed under, through lack of sleep and much reading and writing, but 'twas only to be expected, and the marks disappeared when I was free from strain and fret. My body was as slender as a girl's, my hair as bright, my step as free — nay, I am wrong there. My step was not so free when I walked slow, by reason of a slight limp left by the cursed ulcer that grew when I fell on the boards of Windsor Terrace in 1569. It had healed after a year, but it had left its legacy. If I tramped fast, the limp noticed not, nor did it impede my dancing, praise be to God. In time it vanished altogether and none more grateful than I.

While I was in Kent, the gallant and adventurous sailor, Francis Drake, arrived at Plymouth after a successful voyage to Nombre de Dios in the New World, having captured a huge Spanish treasure-train there. Although all the good folk of Plymouth had rushed out of the church to greet him, leaving the poor preacher mouthing to empty air, I could give Drake no official praise, or even recognition, for Burghley and I, with the help of the Spanish agent, Antonio de Guaros, had set up an agreement with Spain, and trade was resumed. There was no Spanish Ambassador now at my Court, for De Spes had been deep involved in the Norfolk plot and was returned to Spain.

I was right grateful indeed for Drake's plunder, but sent him a secret message to go away and stay away until he should hear from me further, for I did not wish my delicate Spanish negotiations upset. He obeyed and went, none knew where, for a year or two, until he was discovered in Ireland, fighting under the command of my cousin Lettice's husband. He was an extraordinary man, that Drake. A man of my times, of England's golden age.

During the next spring died King Charles IX of France, and he was succeeded by the former Duke of Anjou with whom I had opened marriage negotiations in 1571. I expected little promise of friendship from him. Had he not called me 'an old woman with a sore leg', the arrogant palliard, for all the French Court to hear and snigger at? I had swallowed the insult for policy's sake, but I had not forgotten it. However, he seemed moderate enough, and I decided to let matters run on. Besides, I had other affairs to ponder, for Alba had been withdrawn from the Low Countries and another governor, Don Luis de Resquescens, sent in his place.

Being less of a fire-eater than his predecessor, I thought it timely to send him a warning, saying that he was not to make the mistake of thinking he had to do with a mere woman and a nation of women who would let themselves be conquered by a handful of Spaniards. My father would never have let them go so far, I told the envoy, frowning, and woman though I was, I said sternly, I would know what to do. That should keep Don Luis respectful, I felt. But I pressed it not too far, showing great friendliness to the envoy at his next visit. Sure, he must have been in a whirl, wondering at my intentions. Best to keep him so, I reflected, smiling inwardly.

In the summer, just before I left to go on Progress in the West Country, there arrived Don Bernadino de Mendoza, the new Spanish Ambassador, who was a great help to us in bringing the treaty with Spain to full fruition. I signed it while I was in the port of Bristol. I never saw so many sails and masts, nor heard such swearing neither, except at Court. Those sailors are foul-mouthed, brave dogs, by God! I added several new oaths to my collection, wherewith to shock my Bishops upon my return.

Ah, and when I returned, my cousin Margaret of Lennox came to me to 'beg of my goodness', she said. False-tongued bitch, she hated me and always had. Daughter to my father's elder sister by a second marriage, Lady Margaret fancied she had a claim to the throne. Many nasty tricks had she played me, by Jesu, but was never feared to ask for favours. Her hide was a thick one — to 'beg of my goodness', indeed, when she had called me 'whore' behind my back and cared not who heard! Oh ay, she was always ready to do me a mischief if she could and tried oft enough. Yet I forgave her as oft, for she was my first cousin and of my blood. I never knew much of family life as a young one, and so cherished my relatives if I could. There she stood before me, all in black mourning gown and veil for her murdered husband, Matthew Lennox, who had been Regent of Scotland for a time after Lord

Moray's assassination, and for her dead son, Henry Darnley, the husband, also murdered, of Queen Marie. Old she looked, sad and worn she looked, but her nose was as high as ever and her stare as arrogant, showing mighty little respect in her bearing. Well, she was grandmother to a King, it could not be denied.

'You wish to visit your grandson, King James, do you cousin?' said I, striving to keep my temper, for she ever had the power to arouse it. 'Scotland is a woundy, perilous place to visit, I believe.'

'Ay, but I wish to see the child. I long to do so — Majesty.'

How grudgingly she gave me the title, with a scarce veiled flash of the eye! I stared at her musingly. Mayhap someone would do me the kindness to finish her off in that mountainous country. For sure, she was one who would never learn a lesson, be it pushed under her haughty nose. 'Well, you may go,' I agreed at last. 'I see no reason to refuse you.'

Thanking me as if it burnt her tongue to do so, she backed out of the room, leaving me wondering if I had done aright. And by my father's soul, I had not! No indeed, for instead of going straight up to Scotland, she went to stay at Rufford on the way. Rufford was one of the houses

87

of the Earl of Shrewsbury, he who wed that same chattering Lady Saintlow who was mixed in the business of my cousin Catherine Grey. Lady Catherine had married against my wishes, borne two sons, and died in retirement. What a to-do that had been! Lady Saintlow's tongue had been stopped in time, but now, as Lady Shrewsbury, she had access to Queen Marie, Shrewsbury himself being her guardian. I had forbidden Lady Shrewsbury to have any unofficial converse with Queen Marie, knowing the length of her tongue, but needless to say, the two had become close as barnacles.

So to Rufford went my dear cousin, taking her surviving son, Lord Charles Stuart with her. The October rains were heavy and Lady Margaret was so desperate overcome with rheumatic pains in the joints thereby, that she was forced to keep to her room. And who with her, to chatter there? Why, my Lady Shrewsbury, who had also, by some mighty odd chance, come to Rufford accompanied by her daughter, Elizabeth Cavendish! While the two mammas were gabbing in one room, the young Charles and Elizabeth were playing the double-backed beast in another. He was entangled, 'twas said, into marriage. I can well imagine!

Anyhap, they were swift wed, for the girl

88

was pregnant, of course. And there was Lady Shrewsbury puffing off the fact that her grandchild would be in succession to the English throne, as was indeed so. I was fit to burst with anger when I heard of it, for here was Margaret Lennox at her games again. I raged up and down the Matted Gallery at White Hall, kicking stools out of the way, stamping my feet upon the floor like a very war-horse and yelling some of the sailors' oaths I had learned at Bristol.

'Satan's arse!' I screamed. 'That woman is worse than a flea! Wherever she goes, she bites! And the Shrewsbury losel, she *invited* Margaret Lennox, you say. Burghley? She had the bloody effrontery to *invite* her?' Burghley bowed, his face masklike, as I flung about, ranging from wall to window, snatching up a candlestick and throwing it to the floor, catching up a cushion and casting it from me. 'Lennox means to get the crown into her family somehow. You see it, Burghley? And as for the Shrewsbury malapert, she is nothing but a froward climber, scrabbling for nobility. Belly of Lucifer, what a pair! They shall be brought back to London, and to the Tower they shall go. We shall see how their rheumatism fares there, by Jesu! They know full well that no youth of royal blood may wed without consent of the Sovereign! They shall discover that their Sovereign can bite too. See to it, see to it, my Spirit, be-before I explode!'

Even Rob's Easter gift to me of sixty gold, pearled buttons, together with eighteen pairs of gold, enamelled clasps set on five golden chains, with six rubies in addition, did little to soothe me. Mind, I always loved jewellery. He knew it too. Why, there was that gold armlet he gave me all set with rubies and diamonds with hanging pearls, having in the closing thereof a clock. He gave me that in a handsome case of purple velvet embossed with gold and lined with green velvet. I have it still. If I could rise from these cushions, I could put my hand on it, I dare say. Ay . . . but the effort is too great, too great . . .

They fuss about me now, as I sit here. Kind enough, concerned enough, but not the dear ones I knew. Robert Carey, son of my cousin Henry who died some years back, ay, Robert has asked me what I think of as I sit here. 'I meditate,' quoth I, after a while. And so I do. I have much to meditate upon. 'Tis a long life, a long life . . .

★ ★ ★

A long life in truth. My dear old Archbishop Matthew Parker died in May 1575. He had been chaplain to my mother and she had commended me unto his care. He was a dear man indeed, so sweet and gentle. I had once railed against his marriage, but was forced to agree later that his wife was a worthy woman. He was the worse for it after her death. I missed him sore, admirable, kindly creature that he was.

His successor, William Grindal and I soon fell out, for we could never agree upon religious policy, and after a year I suspended him, for he disobeyed my direct order to suppress certain clerical meetings which I felt would attract too many Puritans. Well, Grindal was too old for the office and Burghley had overpersuaded me in the matter of his appointment. Even Burghley could be wrong sometimes!

Queen Marie sent me a gift that year, I recall; a charming set of collars and cuffs in network which she had wrought herself, she being a rare needlewoman. Fénélon presented them to me and I admired them greatly, wearing them oft. Ho, what trouble this caused among the Lords of the Privy Council! What jealousies and commotions! One would have thought I intended to free the lady merely because I wore her gift. So when she sent me three pretty embroidered caps, I refused to take them at first, but

Fénélon looked so downcast that I felt churlish. Yet I would not have Marie to think she could buy my favour with gifts, for she was ready enough to plot against me, should occasion offer.

'Well then, I will take them,' said I to Fénélon. 'But I pray you tell the Queen of Scots that as I have been some years longer in the world than she has, I have learned that people are accustomed to receive with both hands, but to give with one finger.' Mayhap 'twas grudging thanks, but I had to take care in accepting gifts from such a donor, for motives can be twisted and words forsworn.

★ ★ ★

But what are all these trifles compared with my visit to Kenilworth that summer? There was never another like that in all my life. Ah Rob, dear Rob, you showed your wealth and magnificence to me and to all. Eighteen days I spent at Kenilworth, and every day some new device, some fresh fancy, some further whimsy to delight and enchant me! Robert Dudley, Earl of Leicester, met me and my train, in state, at Long Ichen, some miles distant from the castle. Ay, and there was a gigantic tent raised in which he gave a feast.

That tent, it was so huge that, when taken down, it required seven carts to carry it away, I heard! After the feast we rode the rest of the way a-hunting, and came to the park gates of Kenilworth Castle at eight o'clock of a golden evening on the 9th of July 1575.

'See, my Queen,' said Rob, all smiles. 'This gift does Jupiter confer upon your Highness, to have fair and reasonable weather at your command!'

I laughed, thinking of some of my Progresses when we rode with soaked and collapsed ruffs, cloaks wet through, and all mired to the thighs, loud complaints and groans ringing in my uncaring ears.

I had given Rob Kenilworth Castle some ten years agone, a fine enough place, but he had improved and adorned it until 'twas a very palace. He had a new block built to enclose the three existing sides into a square, and this new block, Leicester's Building, was high and wide with rows of great, tall windows in the very last fashion. I'll admit we gaped at the splendour of those windows, all flashing like enormous diamonds in the westering sunshine. 'Twas amazing sight. And within, why, such riches as caused us all to marvel again. There was a bed, I mind me, such a bed! It was covered and furnished with peach-coloured velvet trimmed with ash-coloured silk in tassels and fringes, all lined with ash-colour silk broidered with pearl and tinsel. The sheets were of linen so fine as silk, and each bore a blue L and coronet in the corner. That bed was for me. The colours were such as I favoured greatly, as Rob knew well.

There were beautiful looking-glasses in all the best rooms and chairs covered to match the beds. Even the night-stools were magnificent, being of quilted black velvet with a pewter pot in each. Glass candlesticks were in all the staterooms, ay, and there was a chess table too, made of crystal squares and precious gems, the whole framed in ebony-wood, the pieces carved in crystal, half mounted in silver, half mounted in gold. I was fair astounded, but it all delighted me, for I loved luxury and the glitter of gold and jewels. Kenilworth was like a treasure chest made into a dwelling, i'faith.

I was happy to meet Rob's sister, my dear Mary Sidney there, with Sir Harry, her husband, and Philip, their beautiful, brilliant eldest son. Poor sweet Mary, she yet wore a veil over her face, for although 'twas thirteen years since she had taken the pox from me, her face was still not fit for the sight of others, nor ever would be. A bitter repayment for her devotion at my sick-bed, indeed.

We had fireworks the next even, and Jesu, it was as if the heavens darkened, the waters surged and the castle shook, while burning darts flew to and fro, beams of stars, streams and hail of fiery sparks lit the skies.

'By God,' said I to Rob, 'do you bring Jove's thunderbolts for a plaything amongst us little mortals? Have you borrowed Thor's hammer?'

And then, I remember that upon one afternoon when I had returned from hunting, there appeared a rustic attired as Sylvanus, the god of the woods, running beside my horse, with music and songs sounding from the bushes. At the close of the songs, Sylvanus snapped the sapling he bore, and cast it from him in token of submission, half of it catching my mount upon the head, making him to rear and plunge, but I reined in hard and all was safe.

'No hurt! No hurt!' I called to those running, alarmed, to aid me. 'Fear not, Sylvanus, your Queen is unharmed!' At which the poor fellow near wept with relief, leaning upon a little lad who supported him. Such eyes the child had, and fixed on me like two lamps. I beckoned him and he came to my stirrup, still staring at me.

'Well, boy,' I laughed, 'and will you know me when next you see me?'

'Ay indeed, Majesty,' said he in a soft Warwickshire burr. 'Who would forget a goddess?'

'Oho, a courtier!' I cried. 'How old are you, my gallant, that you make such pretty speeches?'

'Eleven years, Majesty.'

'A charming age. Can you read and write as well as you speak?'

'Ay, Majesty, I am at the school in Stratford and I like to read and write.'

'What do you write?' I asked him, smiling.

'Why, I could write better stuff than this masque here. I could write a goodly masque of woods and sprites, Majesty.'

'Could you, indeed? Mayhap you will when you are grown. Mayhap you will write one for me, ha?'

'I will, I will!' he promised, those great eyes glowing like stars.

'Tell me your name, then, that I may remember it.'

' 'Tis William, Majesty. William Shakespeare.'

'Well, work at your studies,' I counselled him, 'for that is the way to rise in the world.' I clucked at my horse and he began to prance off. 'Farewell, young Master Shakespeare!' I called to him over my shoulder. 'Mayhap we shall meet again!'

I smile as I recall that pretty incident. That

96

young lad and I, we did meet again. Ay, he is famous now, and a goodly writer indeed. All London flocks to see his plays. The one called 'Twelfth Night' he brought to Court to play for me, and 'twas comical, tragical and exciting all in turn. We laughed ourselves near sick at the steward Malvolio in the play, with his yellow cross-garters and ridiculous posturings. It was a goodly piece that, and others too, writ by the same young man from Warwickshire. England has not heard the last of him, I'll wager.

★ ★ ★

At Kenilworth it rained upon two days, but there was much to enjoy within. Rob had a huge aviary inside the palace, the mesh to confine the birds being of gold studded with rubies and emeralds, and hung between columns all painted with the semblance of huge jewels. It was a sight to open the eyes, I give you my word.

Yea, and on one of the fine days there was a water-pageant, a marvellous doings of a floating island, all glittering with lights, whereon stood the Lady of the Lake. There was a mermaid too, with a great tail, and an enormous dolphin upon whose back sat Orion, the mighty hunter. Coming back from the hunt, I reined in my mount upon the bridge, to watch this magnificent spectacle, all ready to listen with interest to the words of Orion, who stared earnestly up at me from behind his mask, as I sat my white mare. I made a brave sight too, in my orange tawney cloth and my black velvet hat, with its brush of orange feathers at the side, perched upon my red head.

Orion gasped and grunted and bellowed forth some unintelligible sounds. Poor rustic, he had forgotten his lines and was all amazed. At last, he pulled off his mask and cast it aside in desperation.

'Ow! Ar! Save your Grace!' he roared, all crimson in the face with shame and confusion. 'Oi be none of Orion, not oi, but honest Harry Goldingam, save your Majesty!'

Oh, I near expired a'laughing, no matter how I tried to conceal it. 'Twas useless, and I roared nigh as loud as the unlucky Orion. After some struggles, I controlled myself enough to call out: 'Nay, good Harry, be not abashed! Yours was the best part of the play, I swear it. Well done, well done!'

And I charged he be given two gold pieces for my pleasure in his acting and to console him for his distress at mistaking his part.

There was bear-baiting, more fireworks, a party of Italian tumblers who seemed to be without bones in their writhings and contortions, and dancing every night. I had seen and done much in my very nigh on forty-two years, but this was a wondrous visit, and I marvelled at the fantasies arranged for me. Oftimes I found myself near to gawping like a very greenling at the wonders of Kenilworth.

At the end of my stay, Rob escorted me round about the countryside to other great houses, and several time, during our journeys, we ate our food upon the grass under the trees, the food being packed in baskets for the purpose. At Chartley in Staffordshire, Rob took me to call upon Lady Lettice, red-haired daughter of my dear, dead cousin Katey Knollys. Lettice, very pretty and much-indulged, was wed to the Earl of Essex who was my Earl Marshal of Ireland. He, being abroad in that country, had left Lettice to receive and entertain me. She had passed her beauty on to her children, Penelope and Robert, in no small measure; the nine-year-old Robert already showing promise of his future good looks as a man. I found the young ones more charming than their mother, who was affected and self-conscious of her lovely appearance. Also

I noticed that she fixed my Rob with some very languishing stares when she thought my glance was otherwhere. I did not see Rob return them, but he did — he did! Glad am I that I realised naught then, or my happy summer would not have remained a happy memory.

★ ★ ★

Good years they were, those years of the 'seventies. I was in my prime; no longer young, but looking so, my abilities and intellect at their peak. Those held longer than my looks, alas. Well, one cannot rule a country and keep foreign monarchs under one's will upon looks alone, but they help — oh, mightily do they help! A man is ever softened by the appearance of feminine charm and beauty, which is why I exploited both to the full while I had 'em. Now upon my cushions sits a ruin; the dilapidation of the Great Elizabeth, the crumbling of Gloriana. All round me is new, I who was once hailed as the embodiment of the new, the very figure of renaissance. Glorious Phoenix, they called me. Heyday, I am at the end, see'st thou. There is no more for me, I know it. Death stands beside me, but his hand is not yet upon my shoulder. Not quite yet. Nay . . . I will take my thoughts back . . . back . . .

It was in 1577 that I went to Gorhambury, Sir Nick Bacon's house in leafy Hertfordshire. I had visited it some seven years before, but 'twas small then and I had laughed at it for 'a little house'. Very different when I arrived there this Maytime. A new wing, the width of the little house had been thrown out upon the western side, a most commodious, pretty addition. I stayed there for four nights in much happiness and pleasure. Dear Sir Nick, he had a heart of gold — buried in fat, 'twas true — but pure gold for all that. His wife, Anne Cooke of Gidea Hall in Essex, a right learned lady, was sister to Burghley's wife, Mildred, and the sons of the Bacon family were formidable brainy lads. I enjoyed myself greatly, delighting in many a learned discussion in the midst of this brilliant family.

Ay, and that brings to mind the recollection that I had young Nicholas Hilliard to paint my portrait that year. He was, by my royal right, a limner, one who paints in the little, and exquisite miniature works he produced. So, working upon the assumption that one cannot have too much of what is good, I had him paint a large picture. To say him fair, he argued with me over it, saying 'twas not his line o' country and that he was not used to such work, fearing that he would not do me justice. Bloody pox, how right he was! One look at the finished work was enough to send me scurrying aghast to my mirror for re-assurance. The work itself was right handsome, but the subject, dear Heaven, was not. I had worn an elegant, black velvet gown with a stomacher of pearl, pearls about my throat, and my cipher broidered in gold upon the right sleeve. Mine own hair was brushed sleek over a pad and dressed in curls down each side of my face. All well and good. But the face! Christ, I looked as if but barely recovered from a quotidian fever. Pink-rimmed, puffy eyes, pink-rimmed nostrils in a great, lumpy nose that hung low, like a door-knocker, over a little, pale, sunken mouth — by my great father's soul, I resembled something risen from a grave after too long a stay! Jesu, I thought, should those who are yet to live in this world clap eyes upon this picture, they will think, 'what a gruesome old bitch was that Elizabeth Tudor! How her courtiers surely must have lied to her!'

But they did not lie, nor did my mirror, for I was not like that. Not then, anyhap, no matter how I may have changed later. It upset me, nonetheless, and I would stare long into my glass, wondering and fearing. Why, everyone has pink-rimmed eyes, come the springtime. 'Tis after the winter spent mostly in candlelight and with little or no fresh fruit and vegetables; I was no different from anyone else in that, but he need not have painted it! Nay, nor was my face so long — ah, 'twas hideous thing, and I would have burned it had I not paid good money to have it done. In the end, I gave the awful object to Nick Bacon who was begging a portrait of me. 'Twas the only one I had to give at the time, and I must say that he blinked at the sight of it.

' 'Tis poor return for your good hospitality, Sir Nick,' I said ruefully, 'but I have none other to give. I would it were handsomer.'

He stared from it to me, nonplussed, and we both broke into a crow of laughter. 'Majesty,' he gasped at last, 'no matter how this lies, 'twill be an honour to have it. A portrait of the Sovereign, no matter how — '

'Detestable!' I finished for him, and we burst out again in mirth.

' — is,' he laboured on, recovering, 'a signal honour to the recipient, as all the world knows.'

'Well, all the world had best not see *this* image, my good Nick! Hang it, if you must, in some dark corner, well out of sight, I do charge you!'

I hope he did, but I doubt it. I dare swear it hangs in proud view of all to gaze upon with horror and amazement for as long as Gorhambury shall stand.

In later years, Hilliard painted more large portraits of me, but then I was showing my age and he painted me young and unlined as once I had been, following the Italian fashion which showed no shadow on my face. 'Twas kind fashion and all the Court painters used it, by my command. There was portrait of me as the Sun Queen, wrought but a few years back by young Isaac Oliver — or was it Marc Gheeraedts the Fleming? I cannot recall . . . nay . . . Heyday, no matter! In it I wore a fanciful high headdress, with a feather and a diadem, set upon my prettiest wig, the true hair beneath it being white and unruly. My gown was of the most beautiful orange satin, broidered all over with ears, eyes and lips to signify my omniscience. In my right hand was painted a rainbow to symbolise peace, and above it the words: *Non Sine Sole Iris*, which is: 'No Rainbow Without the Sun', for I was that splendiferous planet, see'st thou. On my left sleeve was depicted a serpent in the design of a sphere and a heart, signifying wisdom and prudence. The body of my gown was all broidered with posies, for I loved flowers about me at all times, and the pearls with which I was decked proclaimed my virginity. 'Twas lovely thing; like me as I had been in my youth.

There are those now, who whisper: 'She was never like that! 'Tis all wishful thought and fancy.' They are wrong, but there is no one left to set them right. Indeed, I was like that, but not so plump. 'Tis the only difference. Not pretty, but fascinating, a draw to the eye, a flame of fire and colour; oh, many times better than mere pretty! I would have been no different, could I have chosen my looks.

Now 'tis different tale. My flame is flickering, soon to be snuffed out, my glorious sun is setting. Ah, dire and dreadful thought; let me cast it from me, let me reck not of now, but of times past when my years were still before me.

★ ★ ★

Yea, 1577 was a year of gadding about and visiting. 'Twas then that I went to Sir Tom Gresham's house of Osterley, which I had given him as a thank-token for all the services he had rendered England and me by his financial genius. The place had been owned by an Abbess of Syon, but was full worldly under Sir Tom's hand, well fitted up and seemly. I liked it and was pleased to tell Sir Tom so. He bowed his grizzled head, his bright blue eyes twinkling into mine.

'But stay, Tom, afore your head grows too big for your shoulders,' I said. 'The house is well, but the courtyard is not.'

'How so, Majesty? Tell me and I will change it for your pleasure.'

I leaned from an open window, pointing. ''Tis huge, bleak, ugly space and, to my mind, would be greatly improved by a dividing wall. Dost not agree? Ha, well, 'tis your house and you must live in it, so heed me not.'

After a goodly supper of baked beef, basted with butter and served with a sauce of unfermented grape juice presented in a silver saucer, together with fine white manchet bread, washed down with ale-cheat, I retired to my bed. Poor Sir Tom was in a fret, for he and Lady Gresham deemed me to eat but little of their fine fare, but my appetite was ever poor and uncertain. I assured Sir Tom that naught was amiss and that I had eaten greatly, for me, so he was mollified. My bed was comfortable, my stomach and heart were at ease and, for once, I had no hardship in wooing slumber. Judge then of my feelings when, in the midst of night, there arose a garboily tumult withoutside.

'Sweet Jesus Christ!' I cried, leaping up in my bed. 'What in hell's to do out there? Is it an army or a battle that I hear?'

'Heavens knows, Madam,' answered Lenna von Snakenburg, the pretty, widowed Lady Northampton, who was sleeping on the truckle-bed. 'It sounds like men a-building. Could this be?'

'Oh me, indeed it could!' I groaned. 'Why did I not keep my gob shut? Put your head out, Lenna, and tell them to work more quiet if they value their Queen's soundness o' mind!'

Lenna did as she was bid, but we passed a most restless, disturbed night. In the end, I sent her to share my cousin Kate's chamber and sat up writing policies by candlelight through the remaining hours of darkness. When the day dawned, I looked from the lattice to see the courtyard divided by a handsome wall. I had not the heart to tell Sir Tom of my lack of sleep, for his thought had been only to please me, and the courtyard did look the better for it, no force.

So many memories crowd me. Some comical, some sad, some exciting like the great plan of Francis Drake's voyage of exploration. I had released him from my embargo and allowed him to take ship publicly once more, but charged him to keep absolute silence upon my involvement with him and his plans, for my Burghley hated all pirates mortally and believed in such system of marine law as the world used. So I could not let it be known that his Queen was advocating aught that smacked o' piracy and paying good money to the leader of what might turn out to be a piratical expedition! My dearest Kit Hatton and I talked of it by the hour, for he and I, both, had given £1,000 each towards the adventurous project. There were several other shareholders including Sir Francis Walsingham and Rob. Drake himself had put in £1,000 also.

My friend, the learned and clever Dr. John Dee, had writ a book called *The Perfect Art of Navigation*, and 'twas this that convinced Francis Drake that the voyage was no moon-dream. John Dee had dedicated this book to Kit, who was all afire for the scheme and who fired me with enthusiasm also. John Winter, another shareholder, drew up a plan stating that I, as Queen, was to be made privy to the voyage, but 'twas to be given out that all was to go forward under Licence of the Turks in Alexandria.

Because of Kit's abiding interest in the plan and the money he had laid down for it, Drake eventually renamed his ship for him. It had been called *The Pelican*, but was changed, at sea, to *The Golden Hind*, in honour of Kit, a golden hind being the Hatton cognizance. But that came a little later. At the moment, I told Secretary Walsingham to fetch Francis Drake to me, for I wished to see and speak with him.

I received him at White Hall in the small chamber with the red and yellow tiled floor and the green marble fireplace. In that room my father was wont to sing and play upon the harp, in his elder years, with his fool and friend, Will Somers, for company. Master Drake was a short, stocky figure, strong and muscular, indicative of his body's power. His countenance was fine, ruddy of complexion, his hair fair and tight curling, his beard neat and of a yellow hue. I liked his looks, open and bright as they were; feared o' none he looked.

'Well, Francis Drake,' said I, as he knelt before me, 'up from your knees on this hard floor. I would your help in revenging myself on the King of Spain who has dealt us many shrewd strokes to bring us down. I believe you are the only man capable of this exploit.'

He hesitated, seeming a little at a loss. 'What would your Majesty have me do? I had thought I was to go on a voyage of exploration.'

'Oh ay indeed, Master Drake. Exploration, indeed so. See'st thou, I wish to advance England's boundaries and gain possessions abroad in the New World. I wish, mayhap, to found an empire to rival that of Spain. But I do not rule out the fact that you might encounter a rich merchant ship upon your travels and capture her — even more than one — who knows? At any rate, all your doings will do Spain a vast disservice and England a great one. You understand me?'

He gave an irrepressible laugh, his vivid blue eyes smiling knowingly. 'I understand full well, Majesty. Never fear, I will keep mum as a mute. None shall know of your hand in this.'

'That's my good sailor. Now I shall give you some dainties for your ship. Would you like some silver plate and flasks of perfumed waters to ease the stinks of your journeyings?'

He expressed delighted thanks, and I saw that these things were put aboard for him as well as barrels of dried food and pickled meats. He did not disappoint me, neither, as all the world knows. I own I found it in my heart to wish that I could accompany him on his voyaging, for I have ever had an adventurous spirit and a love of daring-do.

In the end, my Burghley got to hear of my secret doings through a certain Thomas Doughty, a treacherous, forsworn gent who sailed on the voyage and who tried to stir up a mutiny more than once, being greedy and jealous of Drake and my favour to him. Drake executed him at Port St. Julian in the South of the World, near the Straits where Ferdinand Magellan had sailed in 1520. But dear Burghley kept silent, at which I was greatly thankful, for I wished Spain to have no possible hold over me. The great voyage took three mortal years to accomplish, and what wonders had Drake to tell of when he returned! He brought me back a ransom in riches and the possessions of a country on the far side of the New World which he called New Albion, annexing it in my name, and setting up a brass plate there to announce it. Ay, thrilling times, stirring times . . . yet one can never have good withouten its leaven of bad, for my cursed leg was paining me and I was greatly feared that it might break out afresh.

I caused Rob to write more than once to Burghley who was at Buxton Spa, to send me of the medicinal waters as a cure. But so angered was I at the thought of my leg that I felt angered with Rob for knowing of it and writing of it. 'Twas enough for Burghley to go to Buxton — he was martyr to the gout. Lord Shrewsbury was there also, to soothe his gouty hand. Sir Tom Smith, Sir William Fitzwilliam, Mr. Manners and my dear friend Lady Isabella Harington were all there, bathing in and a-drinking of the waters as the Romans had done. But not for me, nay, not for me. I *would* be well, I *would* be healthy. I could not stomach the thought of myself as aught but lithe and free from ills of the flesh. When the tun of water arrived, there grew a rumour that my leg was inflamed again, so I refused to drink the stuff in order to prove that all was well with me, and my leg eased itself of its own. So much for physic!

Ah, and was it not in 1577 that the remarkable house was erected upon London Bridge? That was a marvel indeed, and all came from near and far to gape at it, myself included. It was called the Wonder of London, and with truth. The City fathers had restored the Bridge with great splendour, building a new gate to replace the ruinous and unworkable drawbridge at the Southwarke end, and also a goodly tower of three storeys, full of elegant windows and with a covered way below. Then, over the seventh and eighth arches on the northern side, was reared this house. It was four storeys high, no less, and all of wood, with cupolas and turrets at each corner. There were carved wooden galleries outside the long casement windows, and the panels between all richly carved and gilded. It had been brought over from Holland, in sections, by Peter Moris, and pegged together with the largest builder-pegs I ever beheld. Being brought to the Bridge in pieces, all made ready, 'twas up and done in next to no time. The Londoners dubbed it Nonsuch House at once, for naught like it had e'er been seen in England, let alone London. It was a fine sight and so were the water-works that Peter Moris set up upon the Bridge-foot of the City side. Much needed were they, and who better than a Dutchman to undertake the task, the Hollanders knowing all the ways of water as they do.

My beloved London looked well and wealthy, its people happy and content, so I was contented also.

★ ★ ★

My content was short enough, by God's wounds! In the autumn of the next year I was assailed by the most fearful toothache. I had suffered from pains in the teeth at intervals throughout my life, and those in the front of my mouth had begun to grow greyish, with a black spot here and there, which upset me not a little, for to smile widely now spoiled my looks. Yet I never had one taken out, which was fortunate enough, for most of my friends were gap-toothed. The great teeth along my jaws were black and broken, but these were out of sight and so out of mind until they pained me. And how they pained me that autumn of 1578! Twinges had been flickering since April, but now 'twas torment, and all advised me to have the rotten tooth drawn out. But I was too feared, and each time I screwed up my resolution, the pain eased enough to be reasonable and I felt an extraction to be unnecessary. All to no avail. In December the toothache struck at me like a devil, driving me near out of my wits with the most hellish agony. As all our fool chirurgeons were helpless to ease me, the Council sent the good Dr. Dee abroad to discover some learned physician who might know aught of tooth troubles.

'For see,' I mumbled, speaking indistinctly by reason of the pain, a hugely swollen face, and a cloth about my tortured jaw, 'see ye, John Dee, I will have none of the notion that my teeth must all be pulled, so put any such idea from your head. King Philip has had this done, I hear, and now mumbles toothless, like a dotard, living on naught but slops. I'll swear he looks not such a portrait now — *Ah!*' I broke off with a cry of agony at a fearsome twinge, and Dr. Dee hurried to do his best.

His best arrived in the person of John Anthony Fenatus, a foreign physician of some note, who said, after much Latin confabulation, that if the hollow tooth be filled with fenny-greek, or poppy-juice, and stopped with wax, the tooth would loosen of itself, in time, and I could pull it out with my fingers.

'*In time?*' I screeched, though muffled. 'I can wait no longer. I shall run deranged!'

Sweet Kit Hatton laid his dear hand on my suffering head and spoke quietly to Bishop Aylmer who was by, drawing him behind a screen to talk together. I could not weep nor wail. I was past that. Moan, wordless, I could and did. At last Aylmer came again to me.

'Madame,' he said, 'if I have a tooth pulled out, here in your presence, will you do likewise?' I gazed at him, wide-eyed, over the hand that was clapped to my mouth. 'Madam,' he went on, 'I am willing to have a tooth drawn — perhaps a decayed one — that my example might help your Majesty.'

Such heroism! What could I do? My brave

115

Bishop underwent the operation very boldly, and after that I dared the pincers also. It was bad, I will not lie. While Dr. Fenatus pulled the tooth out, I near fainted with the torment, but afterwards — oh blessed, blessed peace! I slept for near two days and nights, and when I awoke I rewarded my courageous Aylmer with a goodly gift and many admiring words. 'Twas great thing, indeed, that he did for me.

Oh ay, and it was that year that my youngest Grey cousin, Mary, died at Placentia under the care of her stepmother, good Kate of Suffolk. Mary, small, plain and dwarfish, was the last of that ill-omened brood. Her eldest sister, Lady Jane Grey, had perished of the axe in my sister's reign, her next sister, Catherine, was dead these ten years, and now little Mary was off my charge. Those Greys, parents and children, had brought almost all their misfortunes upon their own shoulders and had been a sore burden on mine.

And how could I have forgot the building of Holdenby, Kit's great house near Northampton, that he had but just begun? Sure, my wits are not what they were to have forgot the house where he entertained me with such happiness and pride. Yea, and it was near the same time that he took

116

possession of Ely House on Holborn Hill. He had been after it for a year or two by my let. Bishop Cox, who dwelt there, I did not like, for I thought him greedy and devious, and I warned him that I would have him give up his house. At first he refused, so I had to bring great pressure to bear on him, threatening to deprive him of his bishopric, which was in my hand to do. He was not easy persuaded, Ely being a fine property with a big kitchen garden, seven acres of vineyards running near unto Clerkenwell, five acres of tilling land and an excellent house. Even when Kit had moved himself there, Bishop Cox still opposed him in letters and writings. Natural enough, but I wanted my Kit to have of the best. He was delighted with his new London house and lavished much care upon it so that it became a famous sight. It was easy to reach from the City by way of the Cock Lane Bridge or Cowcross Bridge, both over the Fleet River, and when he had done embellishing his garden wall, folk would walk across the bridges merely to gaze at it.

'Behind that wall lies Hatton's garden,' they would say to their children, staring. 'He is a great man and a favourite of our Queen.'

3

WHAT A MISCHIEVOUS
DEVIL IS LOVE!
1579 – 1582

In January there arrived a gentleman from France to see me on behalf of his master, the Duc d'Alençon, who was a suitor of mine. The gentleman's name was Jean de Simier, and 'fore God, how ardent he was for his master! Such grace, such amorous delicacy as he showed, why, he had my Court gallants open-mouthed and enraged. Indeed, he was a most choice courtier, exquisitely skilled in love-toys, pleasant conceits and Court dalliance. He and his companions set us all a-flame. Me with delight and excitement, Rob with rage and others with green jealousy. My poor Kit was not a-flame, nay, his gentle heart was wounded, and oft he was in tears, taking no pains to hide them upon his cheeks, at which all felt much sympathy. But I could only enjoy it all, for 'twas heady frolic, I promise you. Why, de Simier even crept into my bedchamber and stole my nightcap to send to the Duc as a love-token!

'As well I were not abed and wearing it!' said I, bursting into a laugh.

'Ah, would your sweetest Majesty had been so!' cried de Simier, clasping his hands. 'Next time, next time, *hein?*'

I called him my Monkey because of his tricks and because of his name which was like *Simia*, the Latin word for ape.

'Put him in a cage then, for me,' growled Rob. 'Lock it fast and send it back to France. The fellow is cheap mountebank.'

'Jealous!' I scoffed. 'It doth not become you, dearest. It makes your countenance yellow!'

He ground his teeth, favouring de Simier with a fearsome glare from his black eyes, at which the Frenchman bowed courteously, glancing at me with a knowing smirk. I revelled in this game; 'twas what I needed, for at times I was all too conscious of my forty-six years. It enlivened me, stirred me, raised my spirits and improved my looks beyond measure.

A few weeks after the Frenchman's arrival. I took barge for Placentia at Greenwich. Rob, Kit and Simier were with me, one talkative and merry, the other two heavy as thunderclouds, when a shot was discharged from a small boat, wounding my poor bargeman in the arm. My oath, it was a shock, and all was uproar, the fellow with the gun being apprehended most speedily. He professed himself amazed, swearing it was an accident with many protestations of sorrowful innocence. Well, I finally decided to accept his story, whatever the truth of the matter, and pardoned the man. Least said, soonest mended, I felt. My unlucky bargeman I granted a pension for life, for his wound had been taken while in my service. I could do no less.

Simier hailed me as the most courageous as well as *la plus fine dame du monde*, making a great puff about it all, but I thought that his royal master should be with me. If the Duc really wished to wed me, then he should be at my side, I said. How could I make up my own mind about marriage if I had not laid eyes upon the prince? Within a few days of my making these remarks, Rob took ill and went off to recover at his home at Wanstead.

Full of compunction, I visited him there. I had been hard on him and I did not wish him to make himself ill over it. While I was at Wanstead, a member of my guard fired on Simier in the park at Placentia, deeming him an intruder. Simier thought that the man had been in Rob's pay, for Rob was all against this French match of mine. When I returned to Placentia, my Monkey took issue with me over it.

'*Tiens, Majesté*, it was a plot!' he expostulated. 'A plot to speed me to Heaven and end our marriage-project. I know well who is at the bottom of it — ah, *je le sais bien!*'

The weather being mild for Easter, we were out of doors, walking in the park. '*Doucement, mon Singe*,' said I. 'Quietly now, my Monkey. It is well that we are a little apart from the others when you talk so wild. Who then, is at the bottom of this plot, if plot it be?'

'Why, the Earl of Leicester, *Majesté*. He hates me and my master. He hates France and does not wish you to wed the noble Duc d'Alençon, — or le Duc d'Anjou, to name him correctly.'

I smiled, 'Oh, Simier, I am sure thou'rt wrong. Rob is but jealous, see'st thou, but he would not kill you for it. It irks him, poor Rob.'

'Irks him!' squawked the Frenchman. 'That is good — *très bien, certainement!* Why should he be jealous, I ask myself? He knows well that you cannot marry him, that one, *le coquin!*'

I checked my walking, swinging round to face him. 'What, Simier? Why should he not

121

be jealous? Why should he know so well that I cannot marry him? It has been his constant desire for years.'

'Pah, he is wed already, *Majesté*!'

I was utterly dumbfounded. I knew not where to look, what to say, what to do. My breath seemed to leave my body for a space while a thunderclap sounded in my brain. I gripped Simier's arm tight as a vice and heard him wince, but cared naught for that.

'How do you know this?' I asked in a dry whisper, when I could speak.

'There are few who do not know it *Madame*,' he replied blandly. I stared, mute, and he continued: 'It is a simple matter to keep secrets where there are many houses and large palaces all at a distance from one another. And now the Lord Leicester retires to his bed in a pet because you wish to wed. It is of an impertinence!'

'When was it?' I said.

'*Ce mariage?* Oh, last September, *Majesté*. There was to be a child.'

I swallowed. 'A child?' I repeated with difficulty. 'Who is the lady?' But I guessed before Simier said it. Lettice Knollys. Ay, 'twas she. Wedded by my Rob, bedded by my Rob, and even now, mayhap, giving birth to his babe. Leaving Simier standing,

I walked quietly into the palace and sought my privy chamber. I would have none near me. Could suffer none near me. An hundred heated fancies passed before my inward eye. Cropped black hair, long red hair; brown limbs entwined with white, writhing and tumbling in a rumpled bed. I could almost hear the sighs, the chuckles, the gasps and cries of rapture. Yea. My Rob. He was mine no longer. I closed my eyes and my body shook as if with an ague. Wed, and all knew of it save only me. The blood rushed to my head. I screamed at full pitch of my lungs. Lenna, Kate, Ann Warwick, Isabella Harington, all clustered in a fret outside my door, rushed in at the sound.

'Fetch him!' I yelled. 'Fetch him now, from Wanstead! Drag him from his false sickbed and bring him here now, now, *now*!'

'Fetch who, Madam, who?' they babbled.

'Why, the Earl of Leicester! And tell him to leave *his wife*, that she-wolf Lettice Knollys, behind! I will never lay eyes on her again. See to it!'

★ ★ ★

Well, we resolved it in the end. I was for sending Rob to the Tower, but Lord Sussex persuaded me of the foolishness of such a step. So I had him clapped in the Tower Mireflore in the park at Placentia while I nursed my wounded heart. 'Twas nasty business, for he had recently cozened me, with loving words, to lend him £15,000 and I had done so for love, though I could ill-afford it. But naught was ever too good for my Rob. Nay, marry we could not, for marriage was against my deepest nature, but I had denied him nothing I was able to give. I could scarce believe such perfidy. It was given out that Rob was indeed ill and taking physic there in the tower in the park, and after a day or so he left again for Wanstead, there to stay until I could bear the sight of him once more.

It was well for my self-esteem that my little French Prince arrived on the 17th of August. I was at Placentia and received him there, right apprehensive that he should be as short, ugly and pock-marked as had been noised abroad. He may have been all three, but I did not notice it, for he had that thing about him that appeals to women. Some possess it, some do not. It is the same with ladies too. Indeed, to my astonishment, I found him desirable and with great charm. I reflected that, although I had been beseiged by offers of marriage ever since my accession, here was the first suitor to appear in person. 'Twas doubly soothing after Rob's sad defection.

Monsieur, my little Frog, as I named him affectionately, came to me incognito, with no Ambassadors present to scribble gossip about us in their despatches. He stayed twelve days and, 'fore God, he was ardent enough to amaze me who had suffered such a rude shock to my heart and sensibilities.

I gazed oft into my clearest mirror — that pretty gift bestowed on me by Kit Hatton — seeing my face reflected therein between the alabaster pillars and jewelled posies. I did look well. Excitement and Monsieur's ardour had done much to invigorate me, and I was yet unlined which was amazing at my age. Being summer, there were no puffs under my eyes, God a mercy, for that is ageing enough. My neck and jaw were still firm and I did look much younger than my years which were then less than a month short of forty-six. Fortunate was I indeed. I felt young, also, and this shone through my looks.

Monsieur found me very attractive and 'twas not pretence, neither. I was too wise in the ways of men and the world to be deceived therein. Only Rob had ever done so, and that was because mine eyes were blinded by my love for him and the assurance of his for me. Never before and never again were they so blinded. I believe that the very fact of my being older than Monsieur attracted him — some men are so, and he was one. I revelled in the business, the more so because of Rob, and allowed my little Prince many naughty French liberties with my person which inflamed us both mightily. He could not keep his hands from me. I vow, 'twas like old times and my blood ran fast through my veins that summer. It was so heady that I promised him my eternal love and more besides. I felt almost that I could wed the gallant little rascal.

After he left I was quite despondent, and only momentarily was I cheered when he sent me a small flower of gold with a frog thereon, and within it his portrait with a little pendant, from Boulogne. And my cheer was still further fled when there arose a certain John Stubbs, a Puritan, with a tract writ against the marriage for all to read.

After I had read the tract, I was wild with fury and outrage, for in it, Stubbs proclaimed me too old even to contemplate marriage, let alone child-bearing, 'as all my physicians should know'! Added to this was an inflammatory piece about Roman Mass, the flourishing of idolatry and the silencing of the Word of God in the land; this last as a hit at Monsieur who was a Catholic.

To follow this affront there came a long letter from my dear friend Mary Sidney's eldest son, Philip, who warned me that my suitor was 'the son of the Jezebel of our age, as even the common people do know'. Sure, Queen Catherine de' Medici was Jezebel enough — 'twas good phrase — but I was well aware of her doings, and nor was I proposing to wed her but her son. How dare young Sir Philip presume to preach to me, his Queen?

There was enough preachifying going on as it was. Stubb's pamphlet had begun that. From every pulpit came roars of criticism. I would not endure it. Besides, whether I wedded the Frenchman or no, 'twas policy to have him as a suitor and thus keep France my friend. John Stubbs and his *Gaping Gulph Whereunto England is Like to be Swallowed by Another French Marriage*, would be swallowed in his turn by me, I swore, in a fury.

'God's wounds, this is like to ruin all!' I shouted to Burghley. 'Draw up a proclamation! Say that I, England's Queen, will live and die in Christ. Say that this damned *Gaping Gulph* is a lewd seditious book, showing no true regard for Queen or realm! Get it done quick. I want all copies

127

of the thing seized and burned. Ay, I do — never argue with me, Burghley! And I want Stubbs, his printer and his publisher taken for trial. Do not protest, do as I say, do as I say!'

There was a law, made in my sister's reign, that any who had to do with seditious writings must lose their right hand and thereafter be cast into prison. I used it. Not on the printer; he but did as he was bid for his livelihood, but Stubbs and his publisher, William Page, suffered the penalty at Westminster. I was told that there was a large crowd to watch it, too. There was a fellow with a mallet and a cleaver to do it, I heard. And as Stubb's right hand was severed, he raised his hat with the left, crying: 'God save the Queen!' and the crowd groaned. Then he fainted away and was carried off to the Tower.

Page, the publisher, did not swoon, but lifted high his bleeding right arm, handless, and shouted: 'I left there a true Englishman's hand!' And the crowd cried out against me.

I said naught when told of it, but stared, blank-eyed, like some image. I had allowed passion, chagrin, wounded vanity and evil temper to get the better of me. I am not proud of that episode; it showed the black side of me all too plain. I am my father's daughter, see'st thou, and blood will out. My dear people were enangered with me, their idol, and even friends and loved ones eyed me askance. I was wild in my mind at that time, I admit it. Rob's defection had struck me a fearful blow and dried all my kindness for a while. I had at last to face the fact that this was my final chance of getting a child. I still suffered my monthy courses, which, although always irregular, showed no sign of ceasing, and 'twas known that women of my age had conceived and borne children. Desperately I wanted a babe; I loved children and always had. I wanted mine own — but oh and oh, how I was feared! Yet my need was so great, and the shock I had undergone so severe, that I was willing to wed at last and conquer my terror.

Now, and such a jade was Fate, that when I had, after so long tarrying, decided to wed, along came the cursed *Gaping Gulph* and tore all to shreds. I became nervous and asked the advice of my Council, feeling sure of the support of the Lords. Had they not been urging me to wed for more than twenty years? I guessed there might be arguments, but Burghley, my Spirit, who was all for my marrying, would carry all before him, sure, whether Monsieur be Catholic or no.

So there was a great debate on the 7th of

October, from eight o'clock in the morning to seven of the evening, without the Lords stirring from the room, they having sent the clerks away. What a result! I was horrified. Of the twelve Lords there present, seven were against the match! After much talk, Burghley had persuaded them to speak their minds, but was forced to come to me to say that they wished to give no positive ruling until I had told them my own mind.

'But I do *not* know it!' I cried, exasperated. 'This is why I have asked Council's advice. 'Tis because Monsieur is Catholic, I suppose. Well, no doubt there are ways around the obstacle. Mayhap he would be willing to change. What then?'

Burghley looked everywhere but at me and mumbled something unintelligible, shifting his gouty feet as one who stood upon nails. 'If your Majesty would see the Lords — ,' he suggested uncomfortably.

'Have them in,' I commanded. 'What is the matter with you all?' I asked, as they came slowly into the room, looking as foolish as Burghley. There was a silence as they glanced at one another. Then Burghley spoke again.

'Mayhap your Majesty would care to ask each of the Lords present, individually and privately,' he said. 'You could also ask those who are absent — ' His voice trailed away as he saw by my shocked face that I had understood.

They thought me too old! I could not believe it. Too old. The water filled my eyes and I burst into tears before them all. 'Oh, insulting!' I wept. 'And after so long urging me to wed! I marvel that any person should think so slenderly of me as to doubt that I should marry and settle the Crown in my child! It cannot be too late! Now, after all these years of driving me near crazy with your pleadings of me to wed — now you say I am too old. I am not! I am not!' I sobbed. 'If you can do no better than this, I shall tell you no more. I shall make up my own mind whether to take Monsieur as a husband! Get out all of you! Goky fripperers, begone from me!'

Then, drying my eyes, I called Simier to me, asking him to delay proceedings for two months while I would try to gain my country's support for the match. To tell truth, I was in a whirl and knew not what to do in the affair. I needed the friendship of France right strongly, for matters were growing uneasy 'twixt England and Spain through Drake's successful pirating in the New World. Who knew but what King Philip might send an invasion to our shores to put me off my throne and set Queen Marie up

131

in my place? It could happen. So I needed France for our safety and survival.

Musing to myself, I felt, of a sudden, that I wanted no more to do with Monsieur or marriage. It was all too affrighting and humiliating. I could not continue with it. Yet I had to do some-what to keep France sweet. So I sent Monsieur a loving message to warm his heart, hoping that I could hold France to my side against the might of Spain without committing myself to the marriage. In this I used my head. I meant to draw my suitor on a string for as long a while as possible, in order to achieve my end, and then to let him go without letting go of the goodwill of his country. Such a game of tricks and intellect was better than heat and passion. Oh, indeed it was. When heated I made mistakes, when passionate I acted on impulse, and in so doing had, for a short time, almost lost my people's love.

Ah, and in that year of 1579 I lost poor, dear Tom Gresham, my invaluable man of money. Sure, I could not have done without him in my early, lean years of Queenship, and even now he took an almighty load off my shoulders. 'Twas of a sudden stroke he died, falling plump upon the floor in the kitchen of his new house in Bishopsgate one evening. So very sad, and his fine dwelling but recent completed to the latest fashion. I was greatly upset and joined my tears to those of Lady Gresham, whose shock and distress were immeasurable.

What a year that was, so full of anguish and disturbance. I was glad to be done with it.

* * *

In 1581 the French Civil War was resolved and still I procrastinated over my marriage, but saying loudly and publicly that I wanted all settled over it before I was too old to bear children. My nerves were still touchy and my temper the same, as was shown when Ann Vavasour, one of my Maids of Honour, birthed a child in the Maids Chamber at White Hall. No maid and without honour, she! I had heard rumours of her easiness with men and this proved it. I felt ugly-jealous that she should be young and have a child, wed or no, feeling no sympathy but dislike and anger. Besides, what a name it would get the Court if 'twas known that such behaviour be condoned! I was told that she had screamed out, when the pains took her, that the father was the Earl of Oxford who had once admired me. Well, I sent her to the Tower for her trouble, that same evening, to cool her hot blood. Lord Oxford, far from being ashamed, owned his guilt at once and gave the girl £2,000. So is deceit and lechery rewarded! Sad I felt for my poor Burghley with such a son-in-law, and sent Oxford to the Tower also, for a time, to keep him continent.

A month after this sordid happening, 'twas refreshing to go down to Deptford on the 4th of April publicly to congratulate Master Francis Drake who had returned, some six months earlier, from a voyage around the world. He brought back a world of riches too, and for me, as a shareholder in the enterprise, a personal amount of £100,000! I was enraptured. While Drake had been away, many chests of loot taken from the Spaniards had arrived in England and had been stored in the Tower. Ambassador Mendoza had pleaded, with tears in his eyes, for me to return the booty to Spain, but I pretended not to know what he was talking of. Easy come would not easy go if I could help it!

I boarded the *Golden Hind* with much pomp, watched by great and cheering crowds on land and in small boats on the water. I mind that I wore a white velvet gown trimmed with gold and pearl, the skirts being held out by a new-fangled French wheel-farthingale hoop, vastly discomfortable but most courtly and stylish. Over it, I wore a sleeveless mantle of white velvet bordered with sable, and upon my head a small, high-crowned hat with a brush of orange feathers at the side. It looked well and could be seen afar off, so all could have a sight of their Queen. As I climbed aboard, one of my garters came undone and slipped clean off my leg, falling upon the deck of the ship. The Seigneur de Marchaumont, Monsieur Frog's agent in London, snatched up the pretty gold and purple thing, holding it saucily to his breast.

'Nay, my Lord,' I protested, laughing, 'you must give it back. I have naught else with which to keep up my stocking. Give it to me, rogue, I insist!'

'Ah, *malheur!*' he groaned in affected despair. 'I would send it to my master, *Majesté*. Do but imagine his joy!'

'Oh, very well,' I agreed. 'You shall have it when we return to London.' And I kept my word, for 'twas right amusing nonsense, and would keep France amiably disposed, which was much to the point.

Master Drake gave me a beautiful diamond ornament which had somewhat of the shape of a frog. I took it with grateful thanks, noticing Ambassador Mendoza's round eyes of alarm at its appearance. A frog? Then

135

the French marriage was certain, he thought, with obvious agitation. I chuckled inwardly. Let him guess!

'See, Francis Drake,' I said to my gallant explorer, 'I have a sword with me here. 'Tis an elegant, gilded one with which to strike off your head. Ay, for you have turned pirate, I hear!' Catching his mirthful eye at this speech, my lips twitched and I almost gave a laugh. ' 'Tis disgraceful,' I declared with mock-severity and a slight quiver in my voice, 'but mayhap I will change my mind as to your punishment, for you are a very brave man. On your knees!'

While he knelt, I turned to the Sieur de Marchaumont to ask him if he would invest Francis Drake with a knightood on my behalf. He was only too delighted to do so, seeing in this a definite affirmation of friendship between England and France, and Master Drake rose up Sir Francis, most happy and proud. Full well he deserved it, courageous fellow. He had made his Queen, his country and himself rich as Midas. Wealth begets wealth, and now I had enough in the Treasury upon which to build more. The world should soon view England with awe and respect — indeed, 'twas beginning already.

Before April was out, a Commission arrived

from France of five hundred and fifty gents to arrange my marriage treaty, landing at Dover to be welcomed by the Lords Pembroke and Cobham. From Dover, carriages took them to Gravesend, where they boarded barges for Somerset House. I had passed a proclamation calling all good Englishmen to show honour to the French notables, adding that the penalty for sword-drawing, or the provoking of quarrels at Court, would be punished by death. It was necessary with such a Court of hot-bloods as I had. Only the thought of death would stay them.

I wished to put on a great show for my visitors and had a banqueting house raised, of wood and canvas, in the gardens at White Hall. 'Twas enormous thing, painted outside to look like stonework, and having ninety-two windows. Inside, the canvas was cunningly painted to resemble the heavens, while hanging from the roof were large baskets of fruit, flowers and vegetables in season, all bespangled with gold and silver. In all, we had two months of gallantry and feasting; an impressive display of wealth and power. There were long discussions as to the part and parcel of my marriage and, as I had guessed, none could agree. At last, I decreed that whatever was decided by the Commissioners, the final outcome would depend upon an agreement between Alençon and myself, and I sent him a most friendly letter to this effect, sealing it with wax in which there was stuck a diamond.

He wrote back lovingly, but begging for monies to help pay the troops in Holland, and being now in a position to afford this, as well as happy to keep him in my debt, I sent him £30,000. He was delighted and rightly so, sailing over to England in October for a sight of me. Well, I was pleased to welcome him, and gave him a house at Richmond under the care of some of my trusted Lords. When he came to me at the palace, I received him right lovingly, while he seemed to be in transports of happiness at such favour.

I kissed him fondly. 'I had all the furniture of your rooms arranged to my own taste, and I dare say you recognise that bed, *hein, mon p'tit Grenouille?*' said I with roguish emphasis, at which he bowed with a knowing laugh. 'Ah, but you are the most deserving and constant of all my lovers!' I cried, darting a meaning glance at Rob, now back at Court, who looked quick away, mighty discomposed.

I managed to persuade Monsieur to a service at St. Paul's in order to appease my Protestants, and in order to express my content at his compliance, kissed him on the lips before the whole congregation. That did cause somewhat of a flutter, which I quelled with a haughty flash from mine eyes. I pleased myself, let all remember!

In the gallery at White Hall upon the 17th of November, my Accession Day, with the bells ringing out all over the land, I told Fénélon that he could write a despatch that would make his royal master happy. 'Ay, for the Duc d'Alençon shall be my husband,' I said, with something of a smirk. There was a gasp from those nearby who heard me. Taking a ring from my hand, I turned to my little Monsieur and kissed him upon the mouth. 'That's for thee,' I said, 'and this,' giving him the ring. ''Tis a pledge, my dearest.'

'*Ah, Madame, chérie, chérie* —' he gasped, snatching a ring from his own finger, 'Take this, *ma plus belle! Je suis si ravi, si enchanté! Ah, quel jour de bonheur pour moi! C'est merveilleux!*'

He was enraptured and so was Burghley, he praising God that at last I had made up my mind. Not so Rob and Kit, who were far from being enraptured. Rob was in a fret over it and told me so in no uncertain terms.

'Look to your own marriage,' said I, quick, 'and keep your nose out of mine. *You* have naught to say to me of weddings.'

'Mighty sharp!' he returned. 'Folk will wonder if you are still a virgin that you toy so with your little foreign masterpiece.'

'Oho!' I cried. 'You cannot draw me into quarrels, Rob. Let folk wonder. They will never know. You may cease your stirrings; I know what you are about with your plans to make the clergy preach against my union. You think to act against me for the good of England, ha?' He flushed, attempting to disclaim, but I brushed his protestations aside. 'You may leave England's welfare to me, my Eyes, for that is nearer to my heart than all else.'

'You want your Eyes no longer,' he grumbled sourly.

'Nay,' I said. 'You are my Eyes, my ever-dear Rob. But you turned those eyes upon another and they see not so clear for me.'

I turned to poor Kit Hatton who was standing near, his own beautiful eyes full of tears. 'How now, Kit?' I rallied him. 'Would you weep at my happiness?' Poor love, he looked so mournful that I longed to cast all pretence aside and embrace him then and there, but I had a part to play and must not forget it, for England's benefit.

'Nay, I weep not for your happiness, beloved Queen,' he sighed, 'though I am sore at heart that you should love another.

Do, I beg, consider the grief you will bring to your country. Do remember that it is upon the love of your people that your security rests.'

'I do consider and remember it, Kit,' I replied. 'I never forget it. You will find that your fears are vain.'

But he would not be comforted, nor would my ladies who besought me to study the perils of child-birth at my age. At my age, indeed! I told them roundly to shut their interfering mouths, but recalled it as a reasonable excuse that could be used later.

A few days later, I sent for my little Frog. When he came I told him that I had passed two sleepless nights a-fretting, and that should I pass two more of the like I should end in my grave. 'I am torn!' I cried dramatically, clutching his hand. 'Torn 'twixt my duty as Queen and my feelings as a woman! During these hours of wakefulness I have, with grievous suffering, decided to sacrifice my happiness for that of my people. And I love you so dear! Oh, I am heartbroken, heartbroken!'

To judge of his lamentations, so was he. He tore his hair, wept and wailed — 'twas tremendous scene. When he had recovered somewhat, he asked pathetically for permission to depart from White Hall. 'Oh, nay nay!' I quavered, hands to heart. 'Do not leave me so! My dearest, pray stay — I will wed you, ay, at a more propitious time. Ay, please God! But now my feelings are all a-whirl and I know not which way to turn. You cannot depart now, cruel one!'

So he agreed to stay, remaining for another three months, enjoying Yule and Twelfth Night with us, treated with deference and respect. At last I told him, tearfully, that although I loved him past redemption, I feared that I should die in childbirth, and where would England be then? Yea, I must sacrifice myself on England's altar, I declared, wrung-seeming with grief. He thought me marvellous brave and strong, he sobbed, and what would he say to his mother? Poor little Prince, I had duped him indeed.

On the 1st of February he began his return journey to the Netherlands to continue his fight against Spain, I accompanying him as far as Canterbury, where I wept to part with him. Crocodile tears, I fear, for at that time I was more glad than sad to see him go. But I wished him to go happy and in good conceit of himself. Nor would I allow any of my Court to say wrong of him, for he was of royal blood, sincere in his wish to wed me; I did not wish him heart-wounded. I gave him £10,000 in good money, promising him £50,000 more, telling him that he was to return in two months. Rob and I had a quarrel, in private, over the fact that he was ordered to escort Monsieur.

'You *will* go!' I shouted. 'I have had enough of your impertinence and arguments, and I tell you, you will suffer penalties if you do not show true respect to the person I love best in the world! I mean it Rob! Do not shrug your shoulders at me, insolent! Besides,' and I dropped my voice, 'I wish you to take a secret message to the Prince of Orange to hold Monsieur in the Netherlands as long as may be.'

'What!' he roared. 'You do not wish him back?'

I raised a finger for silence, and pursed my lips. 'Pooh, pooh, pooh!' said I. 'That is for me to decide.'

When he had gone, I retreated to my bedchamber where Isabella Harington, Lenna and Kate awaited me. I stood quiet for a moment, then began to chuckle. My chuckle grew to a laugh, my laugh to a shout. 'Ha, ha!' I cried. 'Monsieur is gone, gone, gone! See, my dears, I dance for joy.' And I footed it round the room, snapping my fingers and singing a merry catch. They were astounded at my seeming change of mood. My merriment did not last, however.

I missed my little Frenchman more than I could have believed possible. When there came a message from Rob about him I was eager to heard of his happiness and safety.

'The message runs,' reported Secretary Walsingham disapprovingly, 'that the Earl of Leicester has left the Duke of Alençon like an old hulk, high and dry.'

'Such impudence!' I snapped crossly. 'The Earl takes too much upon himself. What an unmannerly message! I trust he used the Duke politely.'

'I am certain of that, Madam,' answered Walsingham. 'Although impetuous, he is not a fool.'

'I am not so sure!' I sniffed. 'He is very top-lofty. Always was.'

I felt sad and depressed and astonished to be so. I wrote letters to my Frog and he wrote to me, such letters as to set the Channel afire with their ardour. Melancholy I felt, and more so when I faced the fact that with Alençon had gone the very last flicker of my youth. No more suitors would beg for my hand, no longer could I play my game of marriage. That side of my life was over and done. Jesus, I was an old maid! 'Twas nasty, chilling thought.

Heyday, Bess! I rallied myself. An old maid indeed, but you chose to be so. It was your own will, thou knowest . . . Ay, but there was always hope, gloomed my other self. Always hope. Now it is gone for ever. For ever. For ever.

Resting my head on my hand, I sat mute and still. Suddenly I seized my crimson-dyed quill pen, and drawing a sheet of paper towards me, I began to scribble thereon, sighing oft and deep.

I grieve, yet dare not show my discontent,
    I wrote,
I love, and yet am forced to seem
    to hate,
I dote, but dare not what I ever meant.
I seem stark mute, yet inwardly do
    prate;
I am and am not — freeze and yet I
    burn —
Since from myself, my other self I
    turn.
My care is like the shadow in the sun —
Follows me flying — flies when I pursue
    it,
Stands and lives by me — does what I
    have done —
This too familiar care doth make me
    rue it.
No means I find to rid him from my
    breast,

Till by the end of things it be
suppressed . . .
Or let me live with some more sweet
content,
Or die and so forget what love e'er
meant.

That rhyme said all I felt. 'Twas a tangled string that I could not unravel. My rejection of Monsieur made me more loved than ever in England — it was uprush of sheer relief that the hated marriage was not to be. My Frog was giving noble account of himself against the Spaniards in the Low Countries, holding them away from England. Of a certainty he stood 'twixt me and Spain. Poor little, sweet little Prince! He died of a fever two years later and I suffered a deal of secret misery over it, for he had won a place in my heart that he kept for the rest of my life.

4

LET HIM WHO DESIRES
PEACE PREPARE FOR WAR
1582 – 1586

After Monsieur's departure, there ran a succession of plots all directed against me, and at the root of them all was Queen Marie of Scotland. It was a difficult time, for I felt wretched at the thought of my increasingly elderly and unwed state, and missed the joys of courtship greatly. There was one young knight from the West Country who made the days bearable for me. He had come to Court not long before my Frog left it, and a handsome, brilliant young man was he.

His name was Walter Raleigh and he was a great-nephew of my beloved Kat Ashley who had reared me from a child. She was dead these fourteen years, and I was delighted to have one of her blood at my side, especially one so wondrous vivid and exciting. He had come to report on the progress of the Irish war, but I would not let him go back, for I was greatly taken with the young man, who, together with his dark good looks, posessed an intelligence of mind that was instantly appealing. Indeed, he made everyone else seem dull and used up; even Rob, even Kit. His poesie was beautiful, his spirit fiery, and he seemed fascinated by me which was right soothing. Such daring as he had! Why, in his earliest days at Court, he used a diamond in his ring to scratch words upon a window pane for me to see.

'*Fain would I climb, yet fear to fall,*' I read aloud from the pane, leaning over his shoulder. 'Ha, would you so?' I cried, laughing as I snatched the ring from him and scribed, under his line, words of my own. 'Read that, Walter, and say what you will do now!' I chuckled, provocatively.

Peering at the window he uttered the words I had scratched: '*If thy heart fail thee, climb not at all.*' At which our eyes met, roguish and challenging. Soon after this, he showed acceptance of my challenge by appearing dressed so fine and fancy that all were put to shame, and of course, he became the best hated man in the world, so jealous as all were of him. 'Water' was my pet-name for him, a play upon his own Walter, but there was nothing watery about him, he was all sparkle and vigour. Soon enough I made him Lord Warden of the Stannaries in Devon and Cornwall and gave him a wine licence too, so that he should not want for funds to maintain himself.

Later I allowed him land in Ireland, at Cork and Waterford, and made him Captain of the Guard, following dear Kit. In this post he was excellent, raising the military power of his own West Country to a fine degree. Yet I never gave him a great state post, for he was reckless, far too outspoken and most damnably proud. His brain was a marvellous thing but his nature was not, being tactless and heedless of whom he offended. Materially I gave him all I thought right for such a brilliant gent; part of Durham House in the Strand, overlooking the Thames, also Sherborne Abbey in Dorset, so he became rich and well-pocketed, but in matters of state I considered him a babe and likely to remain so.

Poor Rob now, was always unpopular, and 'twas not all his fault, neither. There was much jealousy over him from the first, and he did his very best to cover his mistakes by charming manners and words, endeavouring to become friendly with all. But it never seemed to take, and oft I felt right sad for him. Although I loved him, he had not the gift of easy popularity. May-hap it was because so many had remembered his ruthless, relentless father and thought Rob tarred with the same brush. No matter what he said or did, there was always one to twist it, or see it wrongly and make much of it. Many others made mistakes, but Rob's were magnified out of degree by most people, it seemed to me. One cannot please everyone all the time, after all. He had begun to show grey in his black hair, and the sharp, clean lines of his face were growing blurred, for he was not so slender as heretofore. His dark face sometimes showed a choleric tinge as if too much blood were there. I reckoned to myself that 'twas all along of being wed to Lettice. She would be enough to age anyone, with her airs and graces, insufferable self-consequence and a tongue that never ceased clacking. The Seigneur de la Mauvissière, the French Ambassador, said that Rob seemed right fond of the She-Wolf. Pooh, pooh to that, said I to myself, hoping 'twas not true, for he was still my Rob, my dearest love and ever would be, no matter who or what came between. He had lost little of his old spirit, however, for he dared to suggest to me that one of his wife's daughters by Lord Essex should be considered as a bride for young King James of Scotland! That idea got no further. Perish the thought!

★ ★ ★

When Archbishop Grindal died in 1583, I was not sorry to see him go. His appointment had not been one of my triumphs and he had left a most unsatisfactory situation behind him, with ecclesiastical law being ignored and the foundations of my religious settlement becoming undermined. Very little thought was needed to determine his successor, for I had the very man in John Whitgift, Bishop of Worcester, also Vice-President of the Welsh Marches, a diligent, courageous churchman and an excellent administrator. He set to work at once, with tact and resolution, and Burghley and I had confidence in him from the first, which was never withdrawn. I had need of good men, for dear Nick Bacon was in his grave these four years and the Dutch question was growing right pressing.

I was owed more than £98,000 by the Netherlanders, who were mighty quick to ask for loans, presenting bonds as security, but tardiness itself in redeeming the same. They were not poor folk, neither. Rather were they growing wealthy through their war. Their seeming poverty was caused by naught but mismanagement, which I found intolerable.

'See ye, my Spirit,' said I to Burghley upon one bright July afternoon as we walked towards the archery butts where I intended to try a shot or two. 'I will wager that all this Dutch war will be turned upon my charge by the backwardness in payment of the United Provinces of Holland. It is my rooted opinion.'

He nodded lugubriously. 'You may well be right, Madam, for as you know, our Treasury is stuffed full of Dutch paper bonds, of which we have great store, rather than good gold which we need.'

It was infuriating situation, and caused solely through foreign muddle-headedness, behaviour I would not allow in my realm. Kingdoms have been lost for less.

As well as this, all was not easy in Scotland, for a Catholic party had been growing under the hand of Esmé Stuart, the Seigneur d'Aubigny, made Earl of Lennox. My invaluable Walsingham had dealt with this in a manner which had led to Esmé Stuart's expulsion from Scotland, after which he soon died of a run in the bowels and the clap, nasty fellow. In August, therefore, I sent Walsingham into Scotland again, to speak sternly to the seventeen-year-old King James, using as excuse the behaviour of his lawless Border tribesmen, to remind him that rulers must rule with the consent of their people and that laws must be kept. Scotland's finances were in a deplorable state, and I straightway received a request for a loan of £300 to keep the King's personal guard in a going condition, such a pickle had the country's monetary affairs got into!

Young James no longer desired his mother's release, for he wished to remain King, having been bred to it, but he was no true friend of mine, reported Walsingham, being proud, ungrateful and contemptuous of me on the instructions of his mother. Here was fine thing. The woman was worse than a canker! France was my ally, yet bound in honour to protect Marie's life, for although she had been Queen of Scotland, she had also been Queen of France through her first marriage. And, although James did eventually come to an agreement of sorts with me a few years after this, he could in no wise agree to his mother's execution. Imprisonment was one thing, condemned death quite another. 'Twas desperate difficult state of affairs, especially as my ally-on-paper, King Philip of Spain was becoming increasingly open in his efforts to bring about her release. Quite beleaguered felt I at times, realising that a war with Spain was likely in the future, no matter how I would try to avoid it.

Moreover, Queen Marie was fathoms-deep in more plots to grab my throne. Would she never cease? I knew the answer to that full well. Never till she rest in her grave. She was my cross; I had to bear with her, perilous, ill-gotten creature that she was.

My life had been in constant danger since my excommunication in 1571, when the Pope had sanctioned my murder 'if undertaken in a religious spirit'. 'Tis ever a wonder to me what men will do in the Name of God! I was only too aware that there were one or two French nobles in Spanish Philip's pay who were all for killing me before the planned invasion of England, thus making the way clear for the Lady of Scotland. My inestimable Walsingham heard of this conspiracy through the secret means of his spies, and Francis Throckmorton, renegade cousin to my dear Nick Throckmorton, was arrested and his papers seized. Ha, they contained lists of Catholic noblemen, a plan of English harbours suitable for the landing of invasion troops, and a packet of infamous pamphlets against me, printed abroad.

Upon the rack he confessed that he had set down plans of the English ports with his own hand, that Mendoza, the Spanish Ambassador, had contrived in the design of the plot and that Queen Marie was in full knowledge of the whole. So to Tyburn and death went Francis Throckmorton and straight back to Spain went Ambassador Mendoza, with a flea in his ear.

I was at Hampton Court when the news of the plot broke in November, and I stayed there near unto Christmastide, riding to White Hall upon a beautiful white stallion given me by Burghley's son, young Robert Cecil. I called the lovely creature Chiaro, that being Italian for Light. I rode ahead of my train with Mauvissière at my side. He seemed amazed at the love my dear people showed for me all along the way, running out to kneel in the frozen, wintry mud of the roads as I passed, calling blessings upon me.

'God bless and preserve you, dearest Majesty!' they bellowed.

'Ruination to your enemies, beloved Lady!' they roared.

'Down with Philip and the Scottish bitch!' they cried.

As we came through Chelsey Village I heard a yell of: 'Bess for ever! We love you! We'll bring you Spanish Philip's head on a pike, Sweeting. Bless your red head!'

Turning to Mauvissière, whose look of astonishment had never left his face since Hampton, I said, with a smugness I could not conceal: 'See you, Monseigneur, it appears that not *everyone* wishes me dead!'

He was greatly impressed and wrote a long

letter to his master. Henri III, describing that journey. It seemed that the King of France could not command such loyalty, even if he would.

Once at White Hall, Queen Marie's keeper, Lord Shrewsbury, came to me in a turmoil, for his wife was behaving most unwifely to him, accusing him of being Marie's lover. This was manifestly untrue, as poor Shrewsbury hastened to assure me.

'Madam,' he said desperately, 'what can I do? My wife is like a wild boar — nay worse! She sets all against me, while 'tis all I can do to keep any sort of peace 'twixt her and Queen Marie, for from being bosom-bows together, they have fallen out and quarrel like two spitting cats. 'Tis more than I can master!'

'Sit ye,' said I, 'here on this settle by the fire. Ay, I know well your wife. All is either honey or turds with her — there is nothing in the mid-line. Now, tell me true, is the Scots Queen your mistress? No quibbling, my Lord!'

'Heaven save me, Majesty!' he gasped. 'I had as soon bed with my harridan of a wife! Believe me, Madam, the sole feeling I have for the royal lady is to put as long a distance between her and me as possible. She is not my sort, Madam, I do assure you. She is a — ' Here he stopped, looking somewhat confused.

I laughed. 'I understand you well, sir. You need say no more. Well, you have done me many years fine service, my Lord, and you deserve some assistance. Shall I, myself, look into the dispute 'twixt you and your wife and give you my disinterested opinion in it?'

Lord Shrewsbury accepted my notion with grateful alacrity, making all family papers available to me, then, drawing upon Walsingham's aid, we drew up a scheme, hoping for a reconciliation between the Shrewsburys. The scheme was acknowledged, but the reconciliation never came about. Meanwhile, I took Queen Marie from poor Lord Shrewsbury's keeping and transferred her to that of little Sir Ralph Sadleir who was a stout patriot and unlikely to be cozened into softness.

In the next summer the blow fell and not from Marie, neither, although I have no doubt she was aware of the business, for King Philip of Spain's agents at last succeeded in the murder of Prince William of Orange. The summer sunshine seemed dark for me as I pondered this dreadful intelligence.

'You see how it is, Burghley . . . Walsingham,' I sighed to my two faithful Ministers, the

157

sunshine dancing on the waters of the Thames outside the windows and shimmering in golden reflections on the wooden wall-panelling and carven plaster ceiling of my private cabinet at Richmond. 'It means that my fear has come true. The defence of the Netherlands rests upon my shoulders, even as I prophesied. Now we shall have to send money and men out there, or the Dutch Protestants will be overcome and Catholic Spain will be hammering at out very gates. It is a terrible loss indeed. Prince William was a brave, strong and true man and we shall all be the worse for his untimely end. We shall be pulled into war, willy-nilly.'

A little before this tragedy, during the previous winter, my Council, in a terror lest aught should befall me through murderous plots of Queen Marie, drew up a Bond of Association which they all signed, pledging themselves, in the event of my death, to prevent Marie from taking the Throne, even unto killing her. Copies of this were sent all over the country, so many seals and names being added that a large trunk was needed to carry them; while at Coventry, not content with seals and signatures, the citizens formed a Loyal Association. I opened my eyes when I heard all this, for whispers of these doings had reached me. They were bound to do so.

Such a burst of loyalty could not be hid.

'Jesu!' I had said to Kit as we rode in the park at Hampton. 'I had best not get murdered then! This Bond is lawless affair; 'tis better I learn not too much of it, say I. Have you signed it, Kit?'

'Of course, my love,' he had answered fervently, leaning towards me as our horses trotted side by side along the river-bank, the wind blowing chill off the steely-grey waters, for 'twas cold, bare December. 'I am not violent, thou knowest, but I would fain speed the Scots Lady with mine own hand, should aught befall you.'

'Hush, you fire-eater!' I laughed. 'This is treason and here am I giving ear to it. Suffice to say that I intend to have Queen Marie moved to straiter confinement yet, under Sir Amyas Paulet. Then, mayhap, we shall all breathe easier.'

But he shook his head, unconvinced. 'None will breathe easier until she is with her Maker,' he said.

★ ★ ★

Within a few weeks I had put my plan into effect and Marie was moved south, back to Tutbury Castle once more, under the care of Sir Amyas Paulet, a strict Puritan and totally

159

incorruptible. I hoped this would hold her quiet for a while, and so it did, but for a short while only. At least I had time to think of Dutch matters. These surely did require thought, for all was at sixes and sevens in the Netherlands. As well as this, King Philip had seized every English ship caught sailing in Spanish waters.

'The rat!' I shouted irately to Burghley. 'Now that he has succeeded in killing the Dutch Prince, he seeks to intimidate me by a braggart show of power! He will not do so, as my name is Elizabeth Tudor! I would I were free of this Dutch business, 'tis poxy nuisance.'

I was astounded when the United Provinces of the Netherlands offered me the sovereignty of their states. I refused it. Most of my Councillors were then astounded. 'Look ye,' said I from my great chair of state at the head of the table, 'I cannot take this realm. It is not mine to take, for now that Prince William is dead, stout defender of the Faith that he was, it is King Philip's land by right of inheritance. How should I then negotiate any peace if I were party to such usurpation? It would mean war, and with England blatantly in the wrong.'

'Nay, surely, my Queen!' cried Rob. 'Would it not be better to rule Holland from London and keep her safe Protestant, no matter what?'

I shook my head, the gold and crimson spangles on my wig flashing with the movement. £450 a year I spent on spangles, and not only for myself, but for my ladies also. It made a brave show. I liked colour. 'Nay, are your ears made of cloth, Rob? I have explained well enough. I want no outright war, although I fear 'twill come in time. When it does, I want no mistakes made and England's cause left unmarred.'

'But what then, will you do?' he asked. 'What can be done, Madam?'

'I will take the Dutch under my care,' I answered, smiling, and glancing round at the intent, bearded faces, bright eyes all fixed upon me, 'and we shall draw up a treaty to the effect. As I see it, 'tis the only solution, though an expensive and tedious one, but better than open war.'

Rob and Walsingham were all for trouncing the Spaniards. Their faces fell at my words; Rob's because he was a hot-head and loved a fight, Walsingham's because he was a Puritan and wished to teach the Catholics that their God was all wrong. Both reasons foolish, to my mind. Well, I signed an agreement whereby I was committed to the upkeep of troops and horse and to the security

161

of Brill, Flushing and the Ramekins Fort. A few days later, Antwerp fell and I was greatly alarmed. However, I continued with the treaty, signing it at Placentia near-unto my fifty-second birthday.

Fifty-two — why it was nigh on old age! Many folk died in their fifties years, one does not expect to live much after, 'tis in the nature of things. Yet I felt not old, nor, amazingly, did I look it. Not yet, not yet . . . Sometimes I thought that mayhap a spell had been put upon me to hold away old age, for although none would believe it, to see me now, in those days I had a true look of youth. Those who were younger than I looked greatly older. Ay, that look lasted until my monthly courses stopped and one or two of my front teeth fell out. I was lucky to remain as I did for so long, yet it made the onset of an aged appearance all the harder to bear.

But where had I got in my thinking? Oh, ay, of the woundy Dutch business. Under that treaty I promised to add further troops and cavalry, this time under a high-ranking captain, and I would send two Ministers to sit upon the State Councils at Brill and Flushing. Dire expense, but what could I do? I was no roaring war-monger. At Placentia we discussed the matter endlessly;

162

the whole Court was full of it. Constantly moving amongst my courtiers as I did, almost never alone, I heard wellnigh every version of the business. While each and everyone decided the affair to their own satisfaction, I took my own way. I sent Drake out on an official voyage to the West Indies as my Admiral, with two of my own ships, and twenty-seven others belonging to private investors. Drake left with secret orders to damage as much of King Philip's colonial property as he could, and to capture the Spanish treasure fleet if possible. I sent Raleigh off to harass the Spanish fishing fleets in Newfound-land Banks and recalled Sir John Norris to organise my troops.

Yea, I was happy to see Sir John again. He was son to one of my dearest friends, a friend made in my young days of peril, Marjory, daughter to Lord Williams of Thame. She was very black-avised, so I called her my Black Crow and did so ever after. Many were the times I visited her at her home at Ricote, seeing her merry amongst her great sons, dear Marjory! There was but little ceremony between us, which I liked well, having enough of that each day at Court. Not that I would wish to forgo ceremony, but a change is good for the spirit.

After much talk and gabbing amongst my

163

Ministers and me, I agreed to assign the command of the expeditionary force to Rob. I felt a little dubious over it, for whilst he was near me he did as I wished, but while away from me became far too independent. He loved power, see'st thou, I could not blame him for that. But he was deep in my confidence and held a high state position, he desired to go, and oh, I still loved him. Not in the way of bedding, no more, but with a love of the heart that would not die. He was like part of myself, the dear knave. I would, and then I would not let him go, havering about it all uncertain. His nephew, that nigh inhumanly perfect young man, Sir Philip Sidney, I made Governor of Flushing, for I knew he was high-principled and virtuous. Yet I hated the whole enterprise. I did not really wish to think or speak of it, but was forced to do so through necessity of making decisions.

I spoke loud enough, though, when I heard of Rob's plans. Walsingham came soft-footed to me one day at White Hall, with the news that Lettice, the bitch, was to accompany her husband, with ladies, gowns, grooms, household articles, servants, even carriages.

'Belly of Lucifer!' I exploded. 'What is he about? Is this the behaviour of a general, that he should go on Progress to lead an army? *What* did you say, Walsingham? Forty-four beds for the kitchen workers? *Kitchen workers?* I'll have him back! See to it my Moor, before he and this great gaullimaufry embark! Get him and that She-Wolf back here at once!'

'Madam,' said Walsingham, spreading his hands, 'I fear Lord Leicester has sailed.'

'Oh, God's wounds!' I cried. 'He will botch it up for sure if she is with him. I pray that he will keep his wits about him and not grow too prideful!'

But, oh me, what a galliard was danced by Rob in the Netherlands! He was treated like a prince, with triumphal arches and fireworks wherever he went, given costly jewels, rare wines and comfits, silks, perfumes — oh, an Arabian hoard of delight awaited him and he entertained the Hollanders in kind, spending vast amounts to do so. None dared to tell me of these merryohs, for they knew I would be enraged. And I was, for I discovered all soon enough. I had told Rob most expressly, before he left, that he was to accept no honours nor titles without my permission, and here he was being addressed as *Your Excellency!* I was furious and sent him a letter to call him to order, but the next I heard was that he had been offered the title of Governor-General and had accepted it!

165

Accepted it without one word to me, his Queen, and in utter defiance of my entire policy! I roared like a lion, I went up like a crate of Rob's own fireworks. I was savage with fury and sent him a letter fit to burn the hand of him who opened and read it. He who opened and read it flew into a panic and tried to throw the blame on everyone else, saying that he had been badly advised by this one and that. Lettice, I'd wager!

Jesu, I felt I could trust no one. What was it about the Narrow Sea that turned everyone's heads as soon as they had crossed it? And the double-tongued Dutch, so to treat Rob as a Majesty when 'twas I who had paid for the whole and stood their protector, not he, the prideful windbag! And the lies that had been told me by mine own courtiers as to his doings! They knew, oh indeed so, but not I! Why, he had even juggled with the rates of pay, raising his own as well as the mens' — 'twas intolerable.

'My God!' I shrieked, choking on my watered wine. 'Let the Earl of Leicester remember that the hand which ennobled him can beat him down to the dust! He is knighting men also, do I hear? Fourteen in one day? Jesu, a sniff of command and he thinks himself Charlemagne! There seems to be not enough room in Europe for the pair of us, I swear!'

At least I had steady support from Cousin Kate's excellent husband, Charles Howard of Effingham, son to mine own loved great-uncle. I made him Lord High Admiral, even as his father had been; I could count on him through thick and thin, dear, good, loyal man that he was and is, for all his fierce, ferocious looks. But, in effect, the Dutch mission accomplished naught but to divert Spanish eyes from goings-on elsewhere. The only glory to England was in young Philip Sidney's unnecessary death, met by his bragadoccio in refusing to wear thigh-armour at the Battle of Zutphen.

Needless to say, he was fatally wounded. But as he lay gasping out his life, he passed his water bottle to a dying soldier, and this was reported as the action of an angel in human form, being taken up by all. Songs were sung about it, poems writ, tales told. He became a popular hero. I daresay it served, in folks' minds, to cover the ill-success of the rest of the venture. Myself, I thought it a foolish and pointless death, but gave him a great state funeral, nevertheless, even though all he had done was to make Walsingham's daughter a widow. Yet mayhap he was in a state of unreason, having but just lost his father and mother in death. 'Twas desperate sad thing. His father, good Sir Harry Sidney, had died in May at the age of fifty-seven, toothless and trembling as he himself had said. Fifty-seven is ripe old age and I prayed that I would continue to live beyond it, for I was but just past my fifty-third birthday. It seemed a mort o' years to me. Mary, Sir Harry's wife, had been my heart's friend since childhood. Sister to Rob, she had wed her husband in a love match, a thing nigh unknown, and they had continued to love one another through thirty-five years of wedlock. Their marriage had been a by-word for devotion and kindness, a mighty rare mating. He seemed to love her all the more for her spoiled beauty, seeing the deeper beauty within, while she worshipped him unashamedly. After his death she pined for him so sore, deeming her life worthless without him, that she followed him to the grave within two months. Sir Philip was devoted to his parents, especially to his mother, so mayhap his loss affected his judgment over the armour.

And so the business staggered on. I could not unmake Rob's Dutch title, 'twas done and I would have to tolerate it. It became apparent that he had no head for finance, neither. I began to think he had no head for anything. Somewhat must be amiss with him so to wreck my careful plans. But brighter tidings came with my pirate knight, Francis Drake. He had returned, that summer of 1586, after having harassed and battered the Spanish Empire so that it shook and trembled. I laughed to hear that Spaniards crossed themselves at mere sound of his name — right amusing! He had also wed a new wife, although had not seen much of her. A great beauty was the new Lady Drake, by all accounts. He showed me a miniature of her, and sure, she was a pretty thing, though liable to run to fat in maturity, I thought.

While all this was occupying my mind, Her Majesty of Scotland was busy a-plotting again, but I knew little of it till 'twas well on, for Walsingham kept all under his secret hand. It began along of a young page of Lord Shrewsbury's called Anthony Babington, who felt it his mission in life to murder me and collect the reward offered by the Guise faction in France for the deed. Queen Marie's mother had been a Guise. I remembered her; a pretty woman and charming. Little did she reck of the trouble her daughter would bring! A man named Gifford was arrested as he disembarked at Rye, and was found to be carrying a letter of introduction to

Marie from Thomas Morgan, her agent in Paris. Gifford was a Catholic whose parents lived near to Tutbury. What better place for the taking of messages and plans to assist in Marie's escape? Being offered a goodly fee by Walsingham, Gifford, seeing his bread buttered upon both sides, thereupon consented to play the part of double-agent, and an ingenious scheme was set up of beer-barrels, each with a watertight container into which letters could be pushed through the bung-hole of the barrel. The brewer, though innocent of espionage, was delighted to accept money from Walsingham's spy Tom Phelippes, for his barrels, as well as from Marie for his beer; money is musical word in any tongue. Phelippes paid the brewer to deliver the barrels to him after they had left Marie, removing the letters she had concealed therein. He was an expert in matters of code and sent all messages, copied and deciphered, to Walsingham, after which he rolled up the letters and replaced them in the barrels.

While at Richmond, I could tell from Walsingham's demeanour that some big egg was about to hatch. 'Come, my Moor,' I said. 'What is it that causes your dark face to smirk so unseemly and your black eyes to dance like those of a child at a feast?' He hesitated, looking somewhat disturbed. 'But

170

me no buts, man,' said I decisively. 'I order you to tell me, Walsingham.'

So he told me all of the plot. I was shocked, amused and sorrowful all at once. 'She is a fool,' I said. 'She will put her head into the noose, whether or no.'

'Oh ay, Madam, we have but to wait. There is Gilbert Gifford to help us; a nasty youth, yet with the face of purest innocence. He hath given me a picture of the plotters, but I cannot retain it for long, or they will suspect. Will you see it?'

When he brought the painting to me I was astounded, for 'twas of six young men whom I knew. 'Why,' I said, 'here is Babington, Barnwell, Abington, Tichborne, Edmund Windsor and Charles Tilney! Tilney is son of a relative of mine, Walsingham. 'Tis monstrous! Well, forewarned is forearmed. Take your painting, give it back to your creature, and I will keep my eyes open.'

It was well that I did, for but a day or two later I was walking, all merry in the sunshine, with some companions in Richmond Park, my hand upon Kit Hatton's arm, when I beheld a familiar face upon the fringe of the group that surrounded me. It was the Irishman, Barnwell himself! I turned my head and favoured him with a long, thoughtful stare. His eyes flickered, his face

171

twitched and he made himself scarce with great rapidity.

'See that man go?' said I to Kit. 'He means me ill.' At Kit's gasp of astonishment and dismay I grinned wryly. 'Am I not well guarded today, with no man near me who wears a sword at his side?' I queried ironically, laughing a little at the absurdity of it all.

By the time that those who were with me had realised the full import of my words, Barnwell had got clean away. I let him go, feeling that Walsingham had matters well in hand, which was indeed so, for Marie was taken from Chartley where she then was, to Tixhall under pretext of a hunting party, while Walsingham's men turned Chartley upside down. Sir Francis showed me the list of English noblemen who had promised allegiance to Marie. I read it, I burnt it, and turning to Walsingham I said quietly: '*Video taceoque*,' which in English is: 'I see all and say naught.' Francis Walsingham made to demur, but I shook my head. 'Let it alone. Concentrate on the rest of the matter. 'Tis best.' He did not like it, but he did my bidding.

Very soon, Anthony Babington wrote to Marie saying that he and his gentlemen had decided to effect the 'tragical execution' of myself after Marie had been set free. She, poor ninny, all haste, all excitement and no sense, wrote straight back by way of her beer barrels, telling him and his companions to kill me first, for then her freedom would come of its own accord.

'So we have her,' I said to Walsingham. 'She is caught.'

'Ay, Madam, like a ferret in a trap. And nigh all done of herself. It is plump within the Act for your safety put out but last year. Her days are numbered, Madam.'

'Nay!' I protested. 'Say not so, Sir Francis! There must be some other way. I cannot have her death upon my shoulders!'

He shrugged his own, bowed politely and soon went off on his own concerns, while I went off to Windsor, just as I had done in the Norfolk plot so long ago, and closed all the ports while Walsingham rounded up the conspirators. On the 11th of August, Marie's secretaries Claude Nau and Gilbert Curll were taken, and three days later Anthony Babington was caught in Great St. John's Wood near Marybone Fields. This wood is right large and thick, but Walsingham's men were everywhere and the tree in which Babington was hiding was discovered soon enough, as were the other conspirators in various parts of the country.

All the bells of England rang for joy and bonfires flared all over the land, but I felt but little of the joy. Rather was I overwrought in my mind, for now it was all too evident that I had to make a decision about Marie. In my heart I knew that there was but one decision I could make that was fair to England and her peace in religious matters. I had held it off for eighteen years as being too terrible to face. Now it confronted me.

I had high words with Burghley over it all. 'Nay, I cannot have her taken from Chartley. Nay, I *will* not have her sent to the Tower — that is out of the question!' I clutched my head in my hands. 'Well, if she *must* leave Chartley, let her go to Hertford Castle; 'tis honourable residence. What? Too close to London? What of Fotheringay Castle in Northamptonshire, then? Too difficult a ride from Windsor, you say? Dear God, what a coil! And I tell you Burghley, when Babington and his friends are tried, I want nothing said to incriminate Queen Marie!'

'But Madam, my dear,' he said patiently, as if to a fractious babe, 'how can this be? She is at the root of all. She is the reason and art of this murderous conspiracy.'

'I know, I know!' I cried. 'But she is anointed Sovereign, ordained by God for her place! She is grand-daughter to mine own aunt, and Burghley, she is next heir to my Throne! She is, whatever we may all say. Oh, what am I to do?' I was distraught, seeing no way out of the dilemma. There *was* no way.

The conspirators were to meet the usual end in such case, being hanged, drawn and quartered. I felt it was not terrible enough. I told Burghley so. 'It should be worse!' I said. 'Worse than that, so that all can see and mark what is the fate of such traitors.'

'Well, Madam,' he replied, ' 'twould be against the law to change the punishment. But there is no need to find anything worse if the executioner takes care to prolong their pains in the sight of the multitude. He need not hurry over the business, see'st thou.'

So I left it, but after Babington and his immediate friends had been despatched, I changed my mind, for their deaths had been fearful and revolting to me at least. Knowing that those young men had been taken down from the rope still conscious, been split open and had their hearts and guts wrenched out before their seeing eyes, was too much for me, I hated it. 'Let the rest of the plotters hang until they be dead!' I said in a suffocated voice. 'Then cut them about if you must!'

I wept, I felt like to vomit, I could neither

eat nor sleep. I missed the wise counsel of dear, dead Lord Sussex; I missed Rob. My Rob, my other self, my Star-twin, he was closer to me than any other, he whom I loved with a love no longer of the flesh, but of the spirit, and all the stronger for that. I needed his beloved company.

I need him still, as I sit mum on my bright cushions by the fire. 'Tis a wood-fire, for I hate the stink of sea-coal which is brought up the Thames from the east coast ports. Mayhap to burn wood is old-fashioned, but I care not for that. How folk can abear coal smoke I shall never understand. But there, this nose of mine was ever sensitive. Any strong scent, even oil of lavender, be enough to throw me into a migraine, while ill stinks I cannot abide. I am thought fussy, but 'tis how I am made. My courtiers are obliged to be well-washed to be near me, for too much sweat is most distasteful to my nose. Sweaty velvet, much worn, is enough to make me retch, and I am quick enough to say so, my oath! So my Court smells sweet by my insistence. There was a delicious burning perfume made up for me, which I still use, of marjoram and benjamin. It kills all other stinks and is most fragrant, subtle and lovely. Mouthwashes too, I insist upon. There is nothing worse than foul breath puffed in one's face when all needed to sweeten it is a compound of cinnamon, mastic and rosemary used regularly. Folk are careless, sitha, and need reminding.

And as for privies — well, in most places they are hellish abomination. Not in my palaces, I see to that. My godson, John Harington, son to my dear friend Isabella Markham with whom I shared imprisonment in my young days, has constructed an ingenious engine here at Richmond for me, clever fellow. He wrote a book of it called *The Metamorphosis of Ajax*, which made me laugh, *Ajax* being a pun on another word for privy, namely a jakes. Some thought it lewd, several called unnecessary, all pronounced it impossible. But I had it made, and 'tis great thing, so clean and tricksy, with a cistern of water, a stone shitten pot set in a wooden seat, and a great brass sluice with a key to set a gallopede of water rushing down to wash all muck away. It works wondrous well and stinketh not; a fine invention! He is good lad, my merry godson. I love him dear.

I shall not need his engine much longer, for my time is nigh. My spirit faints within me, willing me away, and I am becoming too weak to struggle against my certain fate. I pray to God and all His angels that my passing may be easy when it comes, that I may slip away quiet and unknowing. So, on my cushions I meditate and wait . . .

5

THEY ARE RIGHTEOUS
WHO NEED NO REPENTANCE
1586 – 1587

The last of 1586 was miserable and nerve-racked for me. I went to Richmond and stayed there, being loth to hear so many foul and grievous matters revealed and ripped up by Parliament at Westminster. I had small desire to be there present, so Burghley and Whitgift stood for me. My God, I wished not to kill Marie, and so I told a large deputation of Lords and Members of Parliament on a dark November day.

They came bowing into my Withdrawing Room as I stood in a window embrasure gazing out upon the dank and leafless gardens, tree trunks glistening with damp, the leaves soggy on the paths, the sky heavy as a wet counterpane. My heart was as heavy.

I listened to their words and told them my mind. 'I have so little malice to Queen Marie,' I said, 'that it is unknown to some of my Lords here — for now I will play the blab — that I have secretly writ her a

179

letter upon the discovery of sundry treasons, saying that if she will confess them privately by her letters unto myself, she should never be called for them into public question.' At their looks of consternation, I beckoned them near me. 'Hear me, sirs. I would forgive this, her latest treason; even would I die if by my death, I could give England a better ruler. But it is for your sakes I desire to live; to keep ye from a worse! Oh my Lords, I know what it is to be a subject, what it is to be a Sovereign, what to have good neighbours and sometimes most evil-willers. I have found treason in trust and seen great benefits little regarded. These have taught me to bear with a better mind such treasons than is common to my sex — yea, with a better heart than is in some men!

'You laid a hard hand upon me with this Queen. As a prince, I am set upon a stage in sight and view of all the world, duly observed. It behoves me to be careful that the proceedings be just and honourable.' I threw out my hands, the water in my eyes and on my cheeks. 'We must take time to consider. We will pray for guidance. We cannot help but delay upon such a desperate matter, but you shall have, with all conveniency, our resolution delivered by our message.'

My voice broke, and covering my eyes with my hand, I turned again to the window, hearing them murmur, sniff and clear their throats, for I had moved them to tears. After they had gone, I felt quite frantic. There must be another solution than to behead Marie. It was against all my principles and would stain my reputation. Although I had much of my father in me, I did not wish to be thought like him in easiness with the axe. What would folk say, if it should be spread that, for the safety of my life, I, a Queen, could be content even to spill the blood of mine own kinswoman? It was horrible quandary.

Twelve days later, the deputation came once more to tell me that the decision to behead Queen Marie was unanimous. I spoke to its members yet again, pouring out my heart, but I might have said my words to a stone wall. Yet mine was the voice that would authorise the proclamation of Marie's fate, mine the hand that would sign the death warrant, and the blame, if any, would be mine. 'Tis easy to wish to be a Sovereign. The reality is different matter.

'Dearest Madam,' said Burghley, eyeing me with real sympathy, yet inflexible as the rest, 'this must be done before Parliament stands down, otherwise 'twill be called a

Parliament of all talk and no do. It must be done, my Queen.'

Marie was caught and so was I. There could be no turning back, it seemed. On the 2nd of December, when Parliament dispersed, I promised to publish the Proclamation against Marie and did so at once, seeing no other way out. Well, it gave Londoners great joy anyhap, for bonfires were kindled, bells rang and loud were the songs and shouts of thanksgiving. I felt no such merriment. I spent a tense, unhappy Yuletide, living in apprehension of what would happen when Parliament reassembled in February.

Although Rob was back with me for a space, it comforted me not, for he had much to explain and he was sick. Ay, he was, although he denied it. He had changed, my poor love, his fine features had blurred, his hair was near white and he had grown stout and puffy-faced.

' 'Tis but gripes in the belly,' he said. 'Naught to cause concern.'

'But I am concerned,' I answered. 'I think you be not hearty.'

He sighed. 'Well, I have not been so sprightly since I was in Holland,' he confessed. 'I have made such a botch-up there, Bess. I know not if 'twas because I was not quite well, or if I became not well by reason of the dire muddle I have made for you.' He shook his greying head. 'I am sorry failure,' he said despondently, 'and were best out of it all. I thought myself so astute, so able, and all I have done is to increase your troubles, mayhap to drive us into a war with Spain.'

I covered his hand with mine own. 'There now, my dear,' I said comfortingly, 'tell me all. You shall not find me unsympathetic. How could I be to you, who are closest to my heart?'

His face quivered and he seemed like to weep. My bright, proud Rob! Sure, he was sick. I drew his head down to my shoulder. 'We will say no more of it now,' I soothed him. 'There are matters worse yet that press upon me.'

And how those matters pressed. Even at Placentia, through all the Christmas mumming and feasting, I could not feel merry. 'Twas as if the axe hung over mine own head. Monsieur de Belièvre from France and an emissary from Scotland arrived to keep all fresh in my mind. 'Twas but a few months since young King James of Scots and I had concluded a most useful alliance, and now, the arrival of his Ambassador, pressing for the life of Queen Marie, seemed fair to put the alliance in jeopardy. After all, Marie was mother to King James.

'Fear not, dearest,' said Rob to me one day, as I sat glum in my private cabinet, hearing the laughter and music afar off and muffled from the Great Hall, where masked dancing was in progress, 'King James does this for policy, merely. All this trumpeting is but for his honour.'

'Are you sure?' I asked dispiritedly. 'How can you know?'

He stared full in mine eyes, smiling wryly. 'Well, I have spoken to his Ambassador, and — stay your wrath, my love — His Majesty hath writ to me.'

'What!' I cried. 'King James wrote to *you*?'

' 'Tis best, is it not? It would not do to write so to you. 'Twould seem as if you plotted, or some such.'

'Humph!' said I. 'Mayhap. But Marie has writ to me herself, Rob, saying that she has a constant resolution to suffer death upholding the obedience and authority of the Roman church; she penned me requests for her servants, for the treatment of her body after death, and for her burial. It made me weep. Christ, I feel I shall never have done of weeping! My heart is rent to bits over this, and so I tell you! Yet, I say strike or be stricken, strike or be stricken. It has come to that. Is there no way of relieving me of such burden?'

'Well,' said Rob slowly, 'it could be done secretly. Whitgift himself inclines that way.'

'Ay, why not, since it seems obvious to us all that she must die? Must I bear the public weight of it all? 'Twill drive me demented,' I cried. 'Cannot Sir Drue Drury and Sir Amyas Paulet see to it at Fotheringay with poison or pillow, 'stead of outright, open execution? They have charge of her there; it should be easy enough. Why must such a fearsome thing be on my back alone?' And I wept anew, my head on his shoulder this time.

Mine own health was not so steady neither, for my woman's courses were showing signs of drying up and ceasing. These years are no good for women. Some grow fat, some grow man-crazy, some shrewish, some nervous and wretched. I took the last course. The smallest matter upset me, causing tears and migraines. I felt tired, I felt restless. Never an easy sleeper, I grew more wakeful than ever. I seemed to misunderstand the kindest word and fell prey to such glooms and miseries as I had not known since my 'prisoned days at old Woodstock Palace. 'Twas miserable time to have to bear such a load of care, I give you my word.

I struggled with myself all through that January, then suddenly, on the first day of February, I sent for William Davison who was acting as a state secretary for Walsingham while he lay abed sick of the stone, at his house in the Papey, near unto the north-east corner of London Wall. 'Twas along of Lord Charles Howard of Effingham that I did so, for he had visited me that morning.

I was sitting, elbows on knees, chin on hands, on a chair by the fire, my feet on a stool, thoroughly out of favour with myself, when in he tramped, fierce-faced as ever.

''Morrow Charles!' quoth I, over my shoulder. 'Ha, you look as if you have dropped a diamond and picked up a pebble. What ails you?'

'See ye here, my Queen,' he said bluntly, falling on his knees before me, almost in the hearth, 'the English people will not tolerate much more of this suspense; the public temper becometh dangerous. Rumours and alarms are rife and a hue and cry runs from place to place like wild-fire. You must sign the warrant, my dear. There is naught else for it.'

I stared at him long. Then I straightened myself. 'So be it,' I said. 'Up Charles, kneel no more.' Turning to my lady-in-waiting, I beckoned her near. 'Brookes,' I commanded, 'find me that man Davison. Tell him to bring me the warrant. Go now, both of you, and leave me to soil my hands alone.'

Mrs. Brookes returned swift. 'He was walking in the Park, Majesty,' she explained, curtseying, 'and came at once, pausing only to collect his papers. He is outside now.'

'Send him in,' I ordered, 'and take yourself off.'

Curtseying her way out, she ushered in Davison who looked hurried and excited. 'So, you have been out,' I said. ' 'Tis fine morning. Has Lord Howard told you to bring the death warrant for Queen Marie?'

'Ay indeed, Majesty,' replied Davison eagerly, proffering the parchment neatly rolled.

Opening it and smoothing it out upon the table, I drew up a chair, read the thing through and told Davison to fetch me pen and ink. When he had done so, I seized the pen, took a deep breath and, before I could think further, signed it. It was done, but I could not bear the sight of it and cast the parchment to the floor.

'Well, Davison,' said I, 'are you not sorry to see that signed?'

'I am sorry for the necessity of it, Madam,' he answered.

I gave a twisted, downward smile. 'What else have you there for me? State papers? Very well, give them here.' As I signed these documents, Davison stooped to retrieve the warrant. 'Take that thing to Lord Chancellor Bromley for sealing, and get it done as secretly as might be,' I said. 'And while you are on your way, you had best call upon Sir Francis Walsingham at his house. He lies sick, thou knowest.' I went on with a sardonic half-laugh, 'and this will go near to kill him outright, I daresay.'

Staring into space, I tapped my fingers on the table, absently noting the sparkle of my rings in the firelight. 'Davison,' I said seriously, 'I have delayed so long with this warrant in order that people will not think me eager to kill Queen Marie.' He bowed, thinking me done, but I stayed him. 'Surely the members of the Bond of Association could help me here? 'Tis not *whether* the Queen must die, but *how* she must die. You have heard me say that some way should be found to ease me of this burden. Do you not think that Paulet or Drury could take the matter on themselves? I think that you and Walsingham should write to Sir Amyas and Sir Drue and sound them on the business.'

He looked horrified. 'Oh, Madam,' he stammered, ' 'twould be for naught, I do assure you. A waste of time.'

'And who are you to say so?' I retorted angrily. 'I command you to get it done, and no arguments!'

Next day I called Davison to me again. 'The warrant I gave you, Davison, has it passed the Seal?'

'Why yes, your Majesty,' he answered. 'Should it not?'

I felt upset and agitated. All was moving too fast. 'What needeth that haste?' I snapped. 'I did not say to be so quick!'

He went off, looking worried, and I gave myself up to a further day of torment and another disturbed night full of bad dreams. I saw Burghley the next morning and called Davison to be with us. 'I had a dreadful dream last night. William Davison.' I said. 'I dreamed that Queen Marie had been beheaded and 'fore God, this put me in such a passion with you that I could have done I know not what!'

He hesitated. 'Your Majesty,' he said earnestly, 'dost thou truly mean the warrant to be carried out?'

'Why yes, by God, I do mean it,' I answered, 'but I also mean that I feel it should have been managed so that the whole responsibility of so dread an affair should not fall wholly upon myself. That is what I mean.' They did not exchange glances, but their faces grew strangely mask-like. 'What is it?' I enquired. 'Is aught amiss?'

'No, no,' they assured me. All was well indeed, they said, and indeed, I thought myself content to leave it so; yet, even as we spoke together, the death warrant was on its way to Fotheringay Castle. I knew naught of it until four days later when Lord Shrewsbury's son brought the news to Placentia. He arrived just after my departure for a goodly gallop in the fresh air of the Park, so I saw him not until my return.

'Twas while I was a-gallop that I heard the bells begin to ring, here and there at first, then more and more taking up the sound so that the whole atmosphere vibrated with their pealing. I felt such a shock at my heart that I began to shiver, but turned my horse smooth enough, remarking lightly to my companions that we had best go back. Returning to the palace, I took the news stony-calm, but retired to my room as quick as I could, for I felt like to burst. My cries and weeping nigh drowned the sound of the bells, for I grew quite wild. Neither Kate, nor Ann Warwick, nor Delphy Scrope could quiet me. I was like a mad thing, throwing myself hither and yon, calling out and sobbing like one fit for a zany-house.

In the morning, I screamed to Kit Hatton that Davison had betrayed me. The next day, a Saturday it was, I called my Councillors and hurled abuse at them like a very virago. Poor Burghley and Davison had the worst of it.

'Beasts! Traitors!' I shrieked. 'I told Davison to keep the warrant in his hands! I did, I did! Do not deny it! Do you call me mad or a liar to contradict me? Be silent, I say! I did not mean to have it carried out then — mayhap never! You have stolen a march on me, you have wickedly encroached on my power and made me an object of hatred and calumny to the world! Swine! Carrion! Prison is too tender for such as you!'

I had Davison sent to the Tower; I banished Burghley from Court for two months. I told every one that if I wished, I could have Davison hanged without a trial. Mr. Justice Anderson confirmed my belief that I could do so, and I meant to discover what other judges had to say. I could scarce bring myself to read Burghley's letters and flung them about the floor like so much rubbish. I was told that he was abed by reason of a fall from his horse.

'He is well served!' I shouted unrepentantly. 'He has his deserts. His pride was too great and he is fallen. I care not for his pains!'

My ladies tried to soothe me, but I would not be soothed, nor would I attempt to listen to reason. I could not. Any form of reason made no sense to me. My distress at the predicament I was in had blinded me to truth as well as reason. I could not bear it. The weight of guilt and shame, borne all alone, was too much for me. The feeling that this death would cause others, as yet unborn, to judge me as cruel and unkind, as tyrannical, was more than I could endure.

'Tell me how she died,' I besought Kate, for the dozenth time, as I ranged, distraught, about my bedchamber, my withdrawing-room, the Long Gallery, the Audience Chamber, as if to get away from devils.

'But dearest, it will only agitate you further. Let it rest awhile,' urged poor Kate, distressed, trotting at my side.

'Tell me, I say. Tell me again. Go on, speak!'

So once again Kate faltered out the story as told by Shrewsbury's son. That on the 8th of February, between eight and nine o'clock of a sunny morning, Queen Marie walked into the Great Hall of Fotheringay Castle to meet her death on the scaffold erected there. ' 'Tis said she was tall, round-shouldered and corpulent, her face fat and broad,' said Kate, 'yet all declared themselves

192

astonished at her beauty and grace. She wore only black, save for the white veil and the white lace around her headdress, and her face was serene and composed. She spoke in a strong voice, saying that she meant to spend her blood in defence of the ancient Catholic Roman religion. Then she prayed, after which she was helped out of her black robe, standing revealed in a red petticoat with a lace-trimmed red satin bodice cut low at the back.'

I repressed a shudder. Kate paused, but at my nod, she went on: 'She bade her servants not to mourn but to rejoice, for soon they were to see the end of all her troubles, seeming almost to smile as she spoke. Then her eyes were bound, she knelt, putting her head on the block. As she prayed, the executioner's assistant put his hand on her body to steady it, and the axe fell, missing her neck and cutting into the back of her head. '*Sweet Jesu*,' she whispered, but then the axe fell again and the work was done.'

'Go on,' I muttered. 'The rest — tell all.'

'But Madam, dearest, you know it, and 'tis so dire — '

'Go on!' I repeated harshly.

'Well, the headsman took up the head by the hair, which, horrid to say, came off in his hand, letting the head fall to the ground. 'Twas an auburn wig she wore, Madam, her own hair being quite white and cut very short. Her eyes and lips beat for a quarter-hour — '

'Her hair never grew right after she cut it for her escape into England,' I interrupted. 'She had a mass of very long dark-red curls, I heard, and it never grew right after 'twas cut. She took to wigs after that. She will be a martyr. 'Twas good, brave, courageous death. She knew not how to rule, but she knew well how to die. She will be a martyr and I her murderer!' My voice rose. 'Oh God, I cannot, cannot bear it! I hate Burghley, I loathe Davison — I hate them all! I hate myself! *Ah! Ah! Ah!*'

★ ★ ★

Well, I did not have Davison hanged. Even through the mists of my unreason I realised the foolishness of that. Although he was deprived of his office, committed to the Tower and fined 10,000 marks, his imprisonment was right comfortable and lasted but a year, after which his fine was repaid to him. He was not reinstated, but his monies were paid for the rest of his life. But it took Burghley to convince me of all this, once he had returned to Court and I could bear to speak and listen to him. I felt, somehow, that Davison had betrayed me, that I had been misunderstood. Yet now I see that it was not so. 'Tis easy enough to comprehend from sixteen years on, and using the wisdom of hindsight, that I suffered an hysterical collapse and knew neither what I thought, said, nor did. I was out of my mind for a space, with the horror of it and the terrifying heaviness of such a fearful load upon my shoulders alone.

Even though my feelings were in a very riot, I did cause myself to listen to Burghley, for I knew, none better, that he was entirely loyal to me and that his advice had ever been disinterested and sound, so that, in spite of my state of mind, my commonsense had not altogether flown. Although I said no word of apology to him, nor mentioned the business thereafter, I let him know that my heart had warmed again to him, for I paid a visit to his wondrous great house of Theobalds in Hertfordshire. We called it *Tibbals* always, though 'twas writ a score of different spellings, and I still call it so. I remained there for nigh a month — a very long stay. During that time we renewed our love and friendship, returning closer than ever. I see now that I was in danger of becoming a tyrant in my treatment of poor Burghley and saved myself in the nick of time.

6

UPHEAVALS, LAMENTATIONS AND THE RUIN OF EMPIRES
1587 – 1592

But I had let loose the dogs of war with Marie's death. Philip of Spain, quiet enough while she still lived, now began to shake his sword. He had not wished to put the Crown of England upon her head, nay, 'twas for his own he intended it. He thought that all my English Catholics were but waiting to welcome him as King, but he was wrong. No Englishman, whether Catholic or Protestant, wished to see England as a vassal of Spain, and was ready to fight for independence. I knew that a great fleet was a-building in Spain, and that the ships thereof were designed to sail along the Narrow Sea to the Flemish coast where they would pick up horses and troops from the Duke of Parma, Philip's Governor in the Netherlands. Then they meant to make for the mouth of the Thames for a land invasion of England.

A saucy plan which had to wait, for in April, before I went to Tibbals, Sir Francis

Drake had left for Spain and had been raising a high nonny-no there by raiding the harbours of Cadiz and Corunna, burning the shipping therein, thus distressing the Spanish fleet and halting preparations for attacking us. He also captured King Philip's own ship, the *San Felipe*, off the Azores, and brought it back entire, with a cargo of £114,000 of treasure in its hold. My share of this was £40,000, and delighted was I when I received the news of my pirate's return on the 26th of June, whilst I was at Tibbals.

'Drake says he hath singed the King of Spain's beard!' I laughed to Burghley over a letter recounting this news. 'Next time he promises to burn it off altogether!'

'Ay Madam,' said old Burghley, his face creasing into a rare smile. 'Sir Francis is a giant upon the waters. He hath set all the old rules of war at defiance with his fast ships and long-reaching guns. He is the master of surprise attack, seizing his advantage and holding it.'

'Speaking of advantage,' I said, 'what thinkest thou of my appointment of Sir Christopher Hatton as Lord Chancellor? He is a good man, but I feel uneasy over it. Sit ye, for God's sake, Burghley, stand not upon ceremony in your own house, man! I shall have Lady Mildred, your wife, accusing me of worsening your gout.'

He gave me a grateful look that spoke volumes. 'Twas good to be on old terms with him after our dreadful quarrel over Queen Marie. I did not wish to fly to extreme of kindness to him after such extreme of unpleasantness, but for all that, I took comfort in his presence and closeness, although speaking naught of that to him or any other at the time. I needed not to speak. We understood one another.

'He is a good man, Majesty. He hath real capacity — a fine Councillor and true statesman.'

'Well, but he is little of a lawyer. I wonder if he hath the head for such a post. Also I fear that some might term him a mere vegetable of the Court, sprung up at night, for he does enjoy my favour. Indeed it has been said that he danced his way into it. The Chancellorship is great office. I wonder if I have done right to appoint him.'

'Very right, Majesty. He deserves it and will honour it. I am very sure that you will never regret such a Lord Chancellor.'

Nor did I. My first instinct, as ever with state appointments, had been sure. He was perfectly fitted for the post, dear, good, clever, kindly Kit. No one spoke against him as Lord Chancellor after he had held the office for a while, for he proved himself to the utmost and gained respect from all.

There was a young man much at Court these days. He was the young Earl of Essex, stepson to Rob and son to that woman Lettice, by her first marriage. He was very beautiful in face and person, taking after his mother, who was, after all, the child of my first cousin. His hair was of a darker shade than the bright Tudor red, but red for all that. He was cousin to me, therefore, also much loved by my Rob. I could not help but notice him, for he was born to be noticed with those looks, and he had the type of nature, bright, impulsive and intelligent, that would bring him forward anyhap. Besides, I had ever a softness for those of my mother's family, excepting only Lettice. But he worried me a little. There was somewhat about him that swung askew. He had a very bad temper, arrogance poorly-hid and a certain secretiveness in him, causing him to go his own way, despite warnings and orders — a hardness, an almost rash inflexibility. This I sensed under the brilliance and gaiety, but as he was young and of my blood, and because Rob loved him dear, I decided to make him Master of the Horse to try if he could be of value to me and the realm. Being the son of Lettice, he took this to mean that

I would let him do as he pleased, a wrong assumption indeed. However, he was but twenty and there was yet time for him to grow more sober in his judgment. I would watch him and heed what transpired.

In December 1587, Rob returned from Holland for good. He did not look well, nor seem well, I thought, being breathless and easily tired, complaining oft of feverishness and pains. He came to me at White Hall and we talked together. 'Are you happy, my dear?' I asked him as we walked up and down the Stone Gallery, the log fires leaping in the hearths, the gentry of the Court all about us at their concerns, some playing at cards, some at ninepins, all laughing and talking, yet leaving us two alone.

'Happy enough,' he said with a smile, 'but not hearty enough. 'Tis this accursed belly of mine plagues me. To tell truth, Bess, I felt unwell all the while I was in the Low Countries. I was not myself, nor am I yet. But think not this an excuse for my poor doings there. 'Tis not meant so.'

'Speak not of that — give it no mind. I understand, Rob.' I took his hand. 'Are you happy with that — at home, I mean?'

He smiled at me fondly, his hand squeezing mine. 'Well, I am,' he confessed. ' 'Tis not as I had hoped, but sufficient good.'

'She may take some credit for that then,' I said, dismissing the vexed subject abruptly. 'Dids't hear what Pope Sixtus V said of me when he heard of Queen Marie's death? It did somewhat to hearten me while I was so overset, and it had humour in't too. He said: *What a valiant woman. She braves the two greatest Kings by land and sea. It is a pity that Elizabeth and I cannot marry; our children would have ruled the whole world.* What thinkest thou of that?'

'Ay,' sighed Rob. 'He speaks true. But marriage? You are armoured against marriage as much as any Pope, my red-haired brat.'

I laughed, kissing his cheek. 'Ah, that old name! Yet Sixtus is brilliant man, thou knowest. He is younger son of the noble Montalto family, and when but a young friar he met old Nostradamus, the sooth-sayer, who told him that one day he would wear the Papal crown. He laughed and went on his way, but now he is Pope, even as foretold. 'Tis interesting tale. I would Nostradamus were here to tell me the result of the war that *I* foresee is to come!

Two months after Rob's return, the Spanish Admiral, Santa Cruz, died and his place was taken by the Duke of Medina Sidonia — unwillingly taken, I heard. He said of himself that he possessed neither aptitude,

202

health, nor fortune for such an expedition as the Armada was to be. By God, it was to be a great one, for Drake had seen the preparations himself and had said that the like was never before known.

Although lacking in naval skill, the Spanish Duke had great will and powers of organisation. He enlarged the numbers of guns and the amount of shot, and reloaded the ships very thoroughly after Drake's raids. By the time that the month of May had been reached in 1588, he was ready to sail.

'Jesu!' said I to Walsingham. 'Dost realise that this Spanish fleet is twice the size of the whole English navy? My father, who founded it, would turn in his grave! Thank God that Drake's cousin, John Hawkins, does well at his work as Naval Treasurer and the men are well paid. Thou knowest that Drake, Hawkins and Captain Frobisher all believe that they are able to trounce the Spaniards. They should know well enough, I daresay. But I like it not, Walsingham. I do not wish a war. I must continue to strive against it, see'st thou.'

He agreed with his lips, but not with his heart, for he was as set upon a battle as firm as any of my warmongers. Yet he knew that if he did not pay me lip-service, at least, to my peace-endeavours, I would use secret means to gain them, leaving him none the wiser. I had my ways. I could be as devious as he. Indeed, I felt I would go grey with all the palaverings and worry. To my dismay, I found that I had begun to do so! So then, I would not be seen without a wig! That was easy enough. I scanned my face closely for the tell-tale line or wrinkle that would surely accompany the appearance of grey hairs. I found them also, God's curse upon it! Not many, sure, but one or two under the eyes and at the corners of the mouth. Well then, I would not look in my mirror! If I could not continue to enjoy what I saw there, I would not give myself the discomfort of seeing it. I would trust to my ladies ministrations and mayhap view myself from afar, but never closely no more.

★ ★ ★

My cousin, the Lord High Admiral, Lord Charles Howard of Effingham, and Sir Francis Drake had wished to sail southward and intercept the Armada in Spanish waters, but I would have none of that. I feared that the Spaniards might elude our English ships and thus arrive in the Narrow Sea, leaving England defenceless. Charles Howard, whom I had made Commander, accepted my dictum after much grumbling and head-shaking, while gallant Drake did but laugh at my fears.

'Ah, let the Queen have her way!' I was told he had said. 'We will trounce these Espaniolies, these Diegos, wherever we engage them. I'll wager my knighthood on't!'

Well, the whole world knows the story. The great Armada left Spain on the 18th of May 1588 and was sighted off the Lizard in Cornwall on the 19th of July. During the intervening weeks, Lord Charles thrice put out to sea in search of the Spaniards, and thrice was driven back by unseasonal winds, cursing his ill-luck. Upon the 20th of July the Armada lay off Plymouth while the English ships were all in harbour there. But under cover of night, Lord Charles got the ships safely out and to wind'ard of the Spaniards by early of the next morn. 'Tis said that Drake stayed to finish a game of bowls on Plymouth Hoe, with all the galleons in sight, before boarding his vessel for the attack, but I never learned the truth of that tale. When questioned on it, all he would do was laugh and say that he knew we would win!

The fighting on the 21st did little more than to put the enemy to loo'ard and distress two of the best of their ships, but the next engagement, fought 'twixt the Isles of Portland and Wight, was a heavy one. Drake seized the advantage of a change in the wind and flung himself at the enemy, cut off one ship and joined Lord Charles in attacking another. All was going finely when English gunpowder ran out and Lord Charles had to retire for a space, re-forming his fleet into four squadrons in command of Martin Frobisher, John Hawkins, himself and Drake respectively. Upon the 25th, Hawkins and Drake tried to drive the Spanish vanguard on to the Owers sandbanks, wreaking great havoc amongst the enemy thereby, but my cousin and Frobisher were not so successful and the galleons were able to make their way further along the Narrows, but slow only. At Calais, the Armada's commander, Medina Sidonia, heard to his dismay, that Parma's men from Flanders were all unready and he had to anchor off Gravelines in bad weather to await them. That was his unluck.

Lord Henry Seymour of the Downs squadron now joined Lord Charles as a reinforcement, but once again my cousin's ammunition was running out as fast as were his provisions, and soon he would have to seek harbour. So it was essential that the Armada be dislodged as soon as might be. The use of fire-ships was the solution, and Walsingham had authorised the sending of seventy-two barrels of pitch to Dover to prepare the fire-ships there. But Lord Charles decided that to send to Dover would lose much time, and so ordered a fire-ship attack that same night, telling his fellow commanders to ready them then and there. Drake offered one of his own vessels at once, then Hawkins followed suit, while the other commanders did likewise, making eight in all. Men and stores were taken off and the ships loaded with materials to act as tinder, while the holds were filled full of powder and shot designed to explode when the fire was hot. 'Twas a wondrous and superb idea, of a magnitude that had never been tried hitherto. All manœuvres had to be carried out in darkness, calling for marvellous skill and bravery.

Medina Sidonia had guessed that fire-vessels might be used, and readied for this by preparing a defence of small boats equipped with grappling irons in order to catch the fire-ships and haul them inshore. What a fearsome shock did he and his men receive that night, for suddenly, approaching them through the dark, appeared eight large ships, full a-sail, heaving straight towards them, each blazing like a flaming comet from Vulcan's fiery cave! So exact was their formation that the

Spaniards imagined men to be aboard them, but this was not so. Nay, Englishmen and ships were *behind* these incandescent craft, ready to fire upon the Spanish grapnel-boats if necessary. But then, the guns of the fire-ships began to explode among the grapnel-boats, filling their sailors with terror, causing them to falter, break formation and give way to the fire-ships which swept straight down upon the galleons riding at anchor. In their panic and desperation, the Spanish cut line and ran wild before the wind over miles of sea.

The next morning, the English navy came closer, to discover that the Armada was all astray. Some of the galleons had run out of ammunition, two were sent aground and captured, and one sunk complete. Many smaller vessels were so badly crippled as to be useless, and there was no harbour where Medina Sidonia might find refuge, so upon the next day, a Tuesday it was, he led his stricken fleet into the North Sea, hoping to sail right round our island and reach Spain by that difficult and dangerous route.

I was in ecstasies over it at St. James's. Each day, Burghley's clever little hunch-backed son, Robert, brought me the news, and each day 'twas better. 'Did we chase the Spanish up the North Sea, Robert?' I asked. 'Twere best not, I think, for supplies may fail.'

'Ay, Majesty,' answered Robert, 'you are right. We turned back at the Firth of Forth, leaving the Diegos to fend for themselves. Wind and water will do the rest. And, Madam, not a single English ship is lost. 'Tis a miracle!'

'A miracle indeed,' I answered. 'God has worked many such for England and me. But what of the men, Robert? Are the losses heavy?'

'Well, Madam, barely one hundred have been killed in action — 'tis almost incredible — but I am assured of the truth of it. But there are many, many sick of the scurvy, Madam, and many have died of the same. 'Tis foul scourge for which there seems no cure.'

'Then the Spaniards ran North just in time for us,' I said, in wonder at such fortune. English fortune, ay!

'Just in time, Madam, for a longer wait would have killed more of our brave fellows of the wretched scurvy.'

'What is to happen to the fleet since so many sailors are sick?' I asked. 'It seems to me that most of it should be disbanded. Who, then, will guard our Western shores?'

'Sir Richard Grenville will do that, Madam,'

he answered promptly.

'Ha, the fiery Red Grenville!' I exclaimed. 'With his flaming head, 'tis a wonder he was not took for a fire-ship himself! But stay — ' I said, suddenly serious. 'What of the Duke of Parma? He lies just across the Narrows with an invasion force at his back. What if he should seize this chance to come at us now that our fleet is so depleted?'

'We will fight him, Madam,' replied Robert Cecil stoutly.

'All very well,' quoth I. 'But 'tis grave danger, Robert. It will not do to grow complacent over the destruction of the Armada while Parma is still able to challenge us. I must speak to the soldiers and keep their hearts up. I would have done so before, but Lord Leicester reported that the great camp at Tilbury was in too much confusion. Now, go I will, confusion or no.'

So on the 8th of August, at White Hall stairs, I stepped aboard my grand, gilded state barge and sailed downriver with an escort of my Yeomen of the Guard. I was clad all in white velvet, encased to the waist in a silver cuirass of bright armour. When my barge tied up at Tilbury Fort, dear Rob was there in front of all his troops to greet me. I had had my lovely charger, Chiaro, taken down to Tilbury the day before, there to await me, and when I caressed his velvety nose before mounting him, he gave such a loud whinny of pleasure that my dignity was near overset.

Once I was up, a page took the reins and another carried my silver helmet upon a white cushion. Bareheaded, I sat my beautiful Chiaro, the sun shining down upon us, flashing upon my armour and upon the armour of the soldiers. Leaving my Yeomen standing rigid by the Fort, I inspected the captains and military, followed by Rob, Sir John Norris, son to my Black Crow, young Lord Essex and the Earl of Ormonde, which last carried my Sword of State also on a white cushion. I was a very Warrior Queen, and this was the effect I had intended. After the inspection came a prayer, then I rode away to rest at the house of the son of Lord Rich which lay nearby.

Upon the next morning, dressed as before, I returned to Tilbury to speak to the soldiers. Chiaro stood like a statue whilst I cried out my speech in a loud voice, so that as many who could would hear my words.

'My loving people!' I called. 'We have been persuaded by some that are careful of our own safety to take heed how we commit ourselves to armed multitudes, for fear of treachery! But, I assure you, I do not desire to live in distrust of my faithful and loving people. Let tyrants fear!' I shouted. 'I have always so behaved myself that, under God, I have placed my chiefest strength and safeguard in the loyal hearts and goodwill of my subjects; and therefore am come amongst you, as you see, not for my recreation, but being resolved, in the midst and heat of the battle, to live and die among you all, and to lay down for God, for my Kingdom and my people, mine honour and my blood even to the dust! I know that I have the body of a weak and feeble woman, but I have the heart and stomach of a King — and of a King of England too; and think foul scorn that Parma or Spain or any Prince of Europe should dare to invade the borders of my realm! To which, rather than any dishonour should grow by me, I myself will take up arms, I myself will be your general, judge and rewarder of every one of your virtues in the field! I know already that you deserve rewards and crowns, and we do assure you, on the word of a Prince, they shall be duly paid you.

'In the meantime,' I cried, gesturing towards Rob, 'my Lieutenant-General, here, shall be in my stead, than whom never Prince commanded a more noble or worthy subject — not doubting but that by your obedience to my general, by your concord in the camp and

212

by your valour in the field, we shall shortly have a famous victory over the enemies of God, my Kingdom and my people!'

I had struck the right note clear as any gong. The entire camp seemed to explode in cheers and yells, on and on. There stood my Rob wiping his eyes, there stood solemn Walsingham shouting like a boy — all was glorious uproar, and Chiaro did not so much as stir a hoof. Ha, I remember it all so well; near all the words I spoke. I meant every word of it, see'st thou. Each came from my deepest heart and the men knew it. 'Tis said 'twas writ down as I spoke so that none will e'er forget it, that it will live for ever.

Well, so it may. I shall not, that is sure, for colder and weaker I grow as I crouch here. Yet I feel not so feared now, by some strange hap. 'Tis of no use to struggle — nay indeed, I feel too tired to do so. Of late, all has seemed an effort and a burden, which to me is sign that my course is run. God grant I may lay my burden down with ease and grace, as Queenly as I have tried to live . . .

★ ★ ★

On the very day of my speech 'twas said that Parma was already upon the way. Almost

I decided to remain at Tilbury among the soldiers, but Rob persuaded me against that, saying 'twould be discomfortable for me there. So I stayed nearby, in the same house as before, until the 17th of August, when Rob broke camp, for the danger of invasion was past. Spanish gold and heart had both run out together.

Burghley was sunk in gloom over the state of our own Treasury, for the whole business had cost a fortune, including the sailors' pay. In this case, 'twas fortune well spent, and so I told him.

When we left Tilbury I was sore concerned for my Rob who looked most mortal ill. 'Twas his belly again, giving him agony. He wore an ominous, shadowed, careworn expression that worried me greatly. I knew that look. I had seen it before upon the face of my stepmother Jane Seymour, upon that of my little brother King Edward and upon that of my sister Queen Mary. I was feared and could not sleep for my fear. Rob said he was bound for Buxton, there to take the waters for a cure.

Just over a se'ennight later he wrote to me from Ricote where he rested a day or so with my dear friend Marjory Norris, my Black Crow. He asked how I did, saying that he prayed for my good health and long life, dear, sweet Rob. He wrote that he was not in good case, although continuing to take the medicine I had advised. Every word of that letter breathed love and devotion. It was his last to me. I never saw him again.

Ah God, the memory of it pierces my heart like a sword. The tears drip down my cheeks and I sigh and sigh. None can relieve me, for the misery is old, the time has gone with my Rob. And I shall go too. It will not be long, nay, not long . . .

He never reached Buxton, see'st thou, for feeling too deadly sick to continue on his way, stopped at his house at Cornbury in Oxfordshire. There, on the morning of the 4th of September, but three days short of our fifty-fifth birthday, he died of a continual burning fever. He died. My Rob, he died and I not there. He died alone and I not there.

His secretary Edmund Spenser, himself a gifted poet and one who loved Rob, told me the news. I stood dumb and unmoving as stone. I felt as if blasted by a lightning stroke, all my faculties suspended. At last, stiff as an aged crone, my slight limp very pronounced, I turned and sought my chamber. There I sat for some days alone; unable to sleep or eat, unable even to weep. 'Twas a taste of hell. Cold, black and bleak. 'Tis strange; I can weep now, but then — why, my tears dried in my heart's blood, frozen in the ice of my grief.

Always have I been one to weep in sorrow. Tears ease the spirit, 'tis said, and never did I attempt to stay mine. But Rob, Rob — ah no tears could ease that loss, that anguish, that torment of desolation. I was different after, ay, harder, colder, less laughing, for the pain in my heart remained, like a bruise, for ever.

I stayed so long, so silent, so still in my chamber that Burghley had the door broke in and entered, all flurried, with some of the Councillors. They halted, stammering and astonished, to see me seated quiet in a chair, holding a packet upon which I had writ: *His Last Letter*.

★ ★ ★

When I came to myself, I was quick to seize Kenilworth in distraint against Rob's debts, even though he had left me an emerald-set diamond pendant and a rope of 600 beautiful pearls.

'Of course I shall take Kenilworth!' I snapped to Frances Cobham and Delphy Scrope. 'I will not let the She-Wolf get her greedy claws upon it. If she thinks so, she will be unlucky. Mayhap she thinks to

216

present it to her paramour, Sir Christopher Blount! No such fortune! She has wasted right little time amourning her husband, so let her mourn the loss of Kenilworth! *I* gave it to — to' — I swallowed — 'to the Earl and I can take it back, so be silent!'

They were silent.

In November I took up residence at Somerset House. I had announced that the 19th was to be a public holiday as well as Accession Day on the 17th. This was to celebrate the deliverance and victory of England, and three days of jollification burst upon London in which all joined with a will. Tilting, bearbaiting, singing, dancing, mumming, music at every street corner, the racket went on by grey light of winter's day and by flickering torches and bonfires at night. I chose Somerest House for my lodging, for 'twas nearer the City than White Hall, and I could see and be seen with greater ease, for my people wished to look upon me and I on them; to cry our love and devotion in that bond which will be severed only by my passing. I pray they will not miss me too much, dear, brave souls! My heart is England's beyond earth, beyond Heaven itself, no matter how many years or centuries may roll on after me. Mayhap I will watch over my beloved land from Paradise — should I reach it!

★ ★ ★

Well-a-well, the fighting was done, thank God, and I wished for no more of it. There were some who wished to continue the battle, to beat the Spanish Empire in pieces and to make of its King figs and oranges. Raleigh was one such. Indeed, he never ceased to clack upon the subject, but I took no heed of that, for all I wanted had been done. The Netherlands were saved, and with our little corner of the world, the cause of Protestanism was upheld. Spain was off our backs and England had a share in the riches of the New World. 'Twas enough for me. Ay, but not for others, it seemed, for early in 1589 young Essex left my Court in secret, stealing off with the help of Roger Williams, a low-born pip-squeak privateer, to join Drake and Norris on an expedition to Spain to sink what was left of the Armada. This had been the object of the sailing, but Drake's hidden object was more piracy, all unknown to me.

Now of this I was right angry. I had good reason to distrust battle-hungry young noblemen. Such had put me in pickles

218

before — pickles that had needed undignified struggles from which to withdraw. I had forbidden Essex to leave Court and he had flouted me. I sent irate letters and messages to the captains of the expedition with orders to restrain Roger Williams, if he be not hanged already under their authority, and to return Lord Essex forthwith. I was unheeded, for a great to-do had begun at Corunna which was not as successful as could have been hoped. Sure, they captured £30,000 of cargo, but 'twas not enough to cover the expense of the mission, while the Spanish warships I had wished destroyed were still afloat.

Upon the return of Drake and his raggle-taggles, the soldiers and sailors of his force were disbanded, and because my express wishes had been disregarded, there was not enough money to give them their pay. 'Twas prime example of lack of forethought allied to disobedience.

'God's Body!' I raged to Walsingham. 'Now the men will cause a grand fuss, you will see! Broken heads and windows will result!'

They did and more; upsets and disorders going on throughout the year. I put Drake and Norris before a Court of Inquiry, to answer for their actions and disobedience,

219

giving them the length of my tongue beforehand.

'On your knees!' I thundered. 'Below the dais! Look not so at me — eyes on the ground, I say! 'Tis all you are fit to see, braggarts, renegades! You are swollen with vanity, have gone to places more for profit than for service; you have been transported with an haviour of vainglory which has defuscated your judgment, and thousands of good men are dead by your vain and greedy folly. How dare you, sirs! Drake, you will sail no more, for I can trust you no more!'

That was in private. In public I spake loud of 'valour' and 'good conduction', but there was to be no more large-scale piracy — 'twas too difficult to control from England. I bethought me of a better plan and laid it before the Council who were delighted at such cunning. In effect, my plan was to stop and search all ships passing through the channel of the Narrow Sea.

'By this law, my Lords,' I said, 'whenever any doth assist our enemy with help of food, armour, or any kind of munition to enable his ships to maintain themselves, I may *lawfully* interrupt the same, and this agreeth with the laws of God and nature and of nations . . . '

Well, as for God I hoped for the best, while as for nations, 'twas complete new idea for them, coming no doubt as a great surprise, but I intended to be first in this field. I smiled with pleasure at my Council's acclamations and have continued to smile ever since, for the policy worked like a magic charm and made me a deal of money. But I had not discontinued the harrying of the Spanish entirely. Hawkins and Frobisher were constantly a nuisance in that direction, causing much loss in coin and treasure for the unlucky King Philip, pray and fall on his knees though he did. Mayhap his God had secretly turned Protestant, I chuckled to myself!

Yet we lost Red Richard Grenville in a fearsome battle in the Azores which he fought alone against a whole Spanish squadron. His ship, the *Revenge*, lost wind and was grappled, Grenville dying aboard the *San Felipe*. Strange, enough, a mere se'ennight later, a great storm fell upon the Azores, and half that Spanish squadron was lost. So good came of bad, but 'twas sad thing to lose so valiant a brave knight, such true Englishman.

* * *

'Twas not only Grenville whom I lost, neither. My Beloved and trusted old friends were all leaving me through Death's dark gateway. Sir Walter Mildmay, my Chancellor of the Exchequer, had breathed his last in 1589; poor, sweet Blanche Parry, whom I had loved from my childhood, died the next year. Eighty-two she was, and blind, loving me still, fretting for me still. She had been through terror and misfortune with me, through Queenship and power, and now she was gone leaving horrid gap in my heart. Before I could recover from this, there came, two days after, the tidings of the death of Rob's elder brother Ambrose, Earl of Warwick, making me to weep anew. So dear Ann was now a sorrowful widow and more of my childhood memories had gone with Ambrose to the grave.

A week after this, my invaluable Walsingham passed away on the 6th of April 1590. What a dreadful, mourning springtime that was! After Walsingham's death, his brother-in-law, dear Tom Randolph died, and in that same year I lost old Sir James Croftes who had spoke up for me when I was prisoned in the Tower some forty years before. If that were not enough, there died Lord Shrewsbury; he who had been Keeper to Queen Marie of Scotland. Ay, 1590 was a bad year, one of sadness and bereavement as I felt more and more alone.

Little did I reck that at the end of the year I would be bereft of my adorable Kit Hatton! Why, he was seven years younger than I, good, beautiful and true — and he loved me for myself. I visited him constantly in his last illness, staying many a night at his house to be near at hand to comfort him and allay his sufferings. Burghley told me after, that Kit had said that I fished for men's souls with so sweet a bait that no man could escape my network. Oh God, the memories, the laughter, the love of life that he took with him! 'Twas right hard to bear, for dearly, dearly fond had I been of him.

As if to force upon me the fact that I was nigh on sixty years of age and could no longer hope for admirers, Walter Raleigh, whom I had favoured, turbulent and unsteady though he was, played me what I felt was an underhanded trick in 1592, for he seduced Bess Throckmorton, one of my Maids-of-Honour. This, after ten years sighing and pining at my skirt-hem. And for Bess Throckmorton, too! Of all the Maids, she was the eldest and the plainest. I dareswear the slipper was on the other foot; I'll wager she seduced *him* out of sheer desperation! Anyhap, I was piqued and sent him to the

Tower for immoral behaviour. And what if I did play at Dog-in-the-Manger, feeling that if I could not have him, then nor could any other? I was the Queen, I could do as I wished. Besides, I was jealous and upset, for the business had brought home to me the fullness of my years, a mighty unpleasant sensation.

I released Raleigh soon enough, but refused to let him lead the expedition he had organised to the New World. However, I did allow him down to Plymouth, for his stout ships had captured the *Madre de Dios* entering the Narrows, a great cargo ship stuffed full of jewels, spices, silks, carpets, musk, porcelain from Cathay and I cannot tell what all. At Plymouth there was much looting and stealing, booty of £28,000 being filched. Both Raleigh and Robert Cecil stopped this infamous behaviour, recovering £13,000 from the looters alone. As it turned out, £141,000 was fairly got for part of the cargo at Leadenhall Market, and Raleigh as an investor, received £36,000. I took 750,000 lbs weight of pepper, which, through a company, brought me in a yearly £90,000 in good gold — most soothing to the nerves.

I gave Raleigh a charter to maintain his colony at Roanoak in Virginia, a parcel of land in the New World named for me, because we believed gold to be found there. We found it not, and many men lost heavily on their colonial ventures; Raleigh alone being shortened of £40,000 over this chancy scheme. I recouped any loss I had sustained by trading with the East, a far more remunerative affair.

7

HIS FOE WAS FOLLY
1592 – 1601

I have not allowed myself to think much, hitherto, of my Wild Horse of Essex, for it pains and sickens me. I favoured him greatly, see'st thou, bore with his follies and arrogance, his haughtiness and frequent lack of mannerly behaviour because he was blood-kin to me and young enough to be the son I never had. I indulged and forgave him as a mother doth a beloved child. But he was not my child, and I was not his mother but the Queen of England with the power of life and death in my hand. He forgot this, to his ill-fortune, for he never understood me, nor tried to do so.

He nigh on lost matters for me in France by his rashness, irresponsibility and refusal to take advice from those I sent with him. He thought of war as a game, with never an idea of the result of its outcome upon England. Nay, he felt 'twas all laid out especial for him — a backcloth against which he delighted to posture. Too much like Lettice, his mother,

I fear me. I ordered him home, and before he returned, he had the barefaced impudence to knight twenty-four of his followers, thus making them beholden to him rather than to their Sovereign, and cheapening a great honour. Besides, it was my business to make knights, and I wished I had not allowed him the privilege. I did not think he would so debase it.

When I heard of this, I said: 'Lord Essex would do well, methinks, to build his almshouses before he makes his knights. Sure, his knights will need them, for where are their lands and their monies? The world will laugh at him, at me and at these beggarly knights.'

Returned, he wept, kneeling before me, red head bowed, all forlorn. Right pathetic he looked, but I remained unmoved.

'Crocodile tears!' I snapped. 'You are heedless and untrustworthy, and none but lies of honey fall from your lips, my Lord!'

'Oh, Majesty!' he protested brokenly. 'I love you. My fortune is as my affection — unmatchable. You may end my life, but never will you shake my constancy. You can never make me love you less!'

'Tell that to a piss-pot!' I retorted, irritated by his smooth tongue. 'You can make me love *you* less by your behaviour! You waste my money and make a laughing-stock of me and England. I know more of your doings than you imagine.'

'Ah, but did'st know, sweet Lady, that when thou commandedst me home, all the buttons of my doublet brake away as though cut by a knife? 'Twas the sorrow and shame that did it, and good buttons they were, too!' He said this with such mournful eyes and mirthful mouth that I could not forbear a laugh.

'Oh, get up and get out!' I said, half-humorously. 'Do try to behave more seemly.'

I was well aware that he desired a place on the Council and I felt that if given it he might be among those able to control him. He was desperate jealous of Burghley and his son Robert Cecil. He envied their grasp of affairs of secret intelligence and wished to compete with them in this. He had Phelippes, the cipher-master, in his household, placed there by Francis Bacon, nephew to Burghley and son of my dear, dead Nick Bacon. Francis Bacon was very different article, an exceeding brilliant, clever young man. Wisdom's child, indeed, but cold and almost inhuman of feeling. 'Twas said he prefered men to women, both in mind and body. One thing was sure, he was mighty spend-thrift and needed a state position, the monies of which might balance his extravagance, and was using Essex to gain it.

Well, we all fell out over it. I considered Bacon unsuitable for a state post. I mistrusted him, despite the frantic arguing and pleading of my Lord Essex on his friend's behalf. Essex thought me old-fashioned and narrow in my outlook, and told me so, moreover. Lord Essex was always sure that my love for him was greater than it was, see'st thou, and could not envisage not getting his way upon any matter on which he had set his heart, doing his best to beat me down in this argument. Sixty years though I had, I was not to be bullied by a twenty-six year old whipper-snapper still wet behind the ears!

So I left vacant the post that Bacon desired and would not be moved over it. Lord Essex then begged the position of Solicitor-General for Bacon. I was displeased at such persistence and told him so roundly. We sat upon a crimson-cushioned bench in my private cabinet at Richmond, disputing it; he springing up ever and anon to argue in defence of his comrade. 'Look ye, Robert,' I said sharply, 'you do all against my wishes. Even your marriage, three years ago, was without my permission. I do not say I would not have given it, but a Sovereign has the right to know of her courtiers' plans.

'Tis customary for a nobleman to ask. Sir Francis Walsingham's daughter was not a nobody to be taken lightly. As Sir Philip Sidney's widow, she should have had a proper marriage, not a sneaking hole-and-corner affair. 'Twas not seemly. Then there was that wretched business in France — nay, do not interrupt me, I will have my say. Then the fuss about Bacon's being given the Solicitor-Generalship, now more pestering! I begin to wonder what Bacon is to you!'

He sprang to his feet at this, looking outraged. 'He is naught but a friend — why, you calumniate me — '

'Be silent!' I snapped. 'How dare you speak so to me? I know well that Bacon has leanings that are out of true. I know too, that he assisted you to your place on the Council. Did'st think I did not?' I laughed humourlessly. 'You underestimate me, my Lord. Sixty years I may have in my dish, but all my faculties are entire. I am not yet in my dotage. I know of Francis Bacon's doings very well and I deem him unsuitable.'

'But he is brilliant! He has the intellect of ten men. I say he is suitable. You are doing him an injustice to pass him over. He is one in a million!'

'Enough!' I shouted. 'I wish to hear no more of your Brainy Bacon. I am sick of the sound of his name. If you can talk of naught else, you had best go to your bed and sleep off the heat of your partisanship!'

After this came the matter of my physician, Rodrigo Lopez, in 1594. Lord Essex began some sort of kick-up about the doctor being involved in a conspiracy to poison me. I was most unhappy about it all, for I liked Dr. Lopez. However, I allowed Burghley, Robert Cecil and Essex to examine the doctor, for one must not take such rumours lightly, but naught was found to incriminate him. I was furious, thinking that Essex had acted out of spite, and called him violently to task over it, for I loved and was loyal to all who served me in any capacity.

'Rash and temarious youth!' I shouted, when Essex stood before me, his eyes flashing, his face white. 'How darest thou enter into a matter against a poor man whose wrongdoing you cannot prove!'

'Cannot prove?' he roared back at me. 'We shall see what I cannot prove, Madam, and yarely!' And flinging round, he dashed from the chamber, clapping the door to behind him with a resounding crash.

I turned to Kitty Huntingdon, who stood open-mouthed by my chair in company with my cousin Kate. 'Christ,' I said wearily. 'I am growing too old for these youthful tantrums. He is worse than one of Drake's new cannons!'

'Let us hope not as dangerous, dearest,' said Kate somewhat tartly. 'Woe worth him if he causes you too much dismay.'

'Do you think he is like to?'

'Ay, I do,' replied Kate. 'In some sort or other.'

'But he is so sweetly handsome, for all that,' sighed Kitty. 'If I were twenty years younger — '

'Oh, Kitty!' I laughed. 'You never change. You should be 'shamed of yourself with such a roving eye at your age.'

'Once a Dudley, always a Dudley!' she retorted with such a saucy look that she set us all a-giggle like silly young girls.

★ ★ ★

Lord Essex was on his mettle to prove Dr. Lopez guilty after that argument with me, for he felt his honour to be involved. It was then discovered that Lopez had indeed had dealings with Philip of Spain, but whether to encompass my death could not be determined. The unlucky Lopez was brought for trial and condemned, but I ordered the Lieutenant of the Tower not to surrender him for execution. I wished

232

to go into the matter more fully in my own time. Two months later, I was upset and infuriated to find that Essex, by secret means, had got Lopez out of the Tower and thus out of my protection, by using his powers as a Privy Councillor to press the judges to have the poor man executed. Beside myself with anger at such dealings, I had another monstrous scene with his Lordship. 'Twas like some horrid game we were playing!

But he was talented and gifted beyond the ordinary, see'st thou, full of energy and fire, and I believed I could use these gifts to help me. Believed so at first, anyhap. I was fond of him, he was of my blood and I felt I should give him every chance to prove himself.

My mouth full of marchpane, I pondered the problem of Essex, which was difficult puzzle, for sure. The marchpane was good. I called for more and some suckets and comfits also. My passion for sweetmeats had so grown with the years that oft I felt fain to dispense with food entirely and subsist wholly upon sweetmeats. But I restrained myself as far as I was able, for I detested extremes, even in appetite. I turned to Delphy Scrope who was stitching near at hand.

'How dost envisage Heaven?' I asked her suddenly.

'Why — why — a place of exceeding beauty,' she answered, somewhat at a loss.

'Well, is that all? 'Tis vague enough. Have you not thought of it and what you would find there?'

'Perhaps sunshine and flowers?' she hazarded. 'Angels with harps of gold? Fountains and trees? Mountain peaks? Jewels?'

I nodded. 'Mayhap. I tell you, Delphy, in my Heaven the mountains would be all of sweetmeats, the fountains would run honey, the trees hang with comfits of marchpane and I would cram myself stupid.'

She gave a shriek of laughter. 'Oh, cousin, *what* a fancy! How your stomach would rue it!'

'I doubt if one suffers the belly-ache in Heaven,' said I, grinning wide enough to show my blackened gap-teeth before I remembered to cover my lips with my hand. I had lost several teeth on the left side of my mouth, which made my speech somewhat indistinct when I spoke fast, but 'twas only foreigners who found it so. Yet my back was as straight and I was as sprightly active as ever, my figure as good. I knew that my face was wrinkled, but my skin was still milk-white and flawless. White, too, was my hair, but I covered that with wigs of

234

a handsome dark red, made by my silk-woman, Dorothy Spekarde, all of different styles and curls, jewelled and spangled. My nose looked longer, for my eyes had become a trifle sunken and my cheeks a little fallen in. Indeed, my nose, when I caught sight of it by accident in some mirror, seemed right beak-like, but there, an aquiline nose is much admired and envied, so I cared not too much, provided I peered not too close. Heigh-ho, age will have us all and wreak his weary will upon us if so be we die not young!

In public, my extravagance in fashion took the eye from my fading looks, or so I hoped. My bodices were of the stiffest and longest, my farthingales the widest, my ruffs and sleeves the largest, my jewels the most multitudinous. I proclaimed my status, my singularity, my power, richness and royalty by my appearance. It certainly impressed all who saw me. However, in private I wore simple gowns and loose robes, for after thirty-six years of pleasing myself in matters of appearance and allowing my fancy free rein, I had grown tired of all the time spent in hooking, lacing, tying, fitting and buttoning required to present a stupendous aspect with which to amaze all beholders. Now I tricked myself out like a peacock only when I was to be stared at, or when my portrait was to be painted. One grows used to most things in time . . .

But Essex! A strange lad was he. He had no enemies, for his charm and popularity were great, and I was his best friend, wishful to help him to find a place that would suit him. Yet his behaviour threatened to lose him all. He was generous, wanting to benefit his friends, and asking my help in this. If I did so, however, he bragged to the heavens that he had but to speak and I would eat from his hand, while if I denied him, he spoke of me as deceitful and treacherous, accusing others of working against him, also. He could conceal nothing, carrying his love and his hatred on his forehead. His enemy was his own self and he knew it not. But still I felt I could control him and put him to good use eventually, as I had done with so many lively young sprigs. He was mad for military doings and had some gift for such, too, so I thought he should be given a military post, pondering this to myself.

No matter what he said to the contrary, I liked not his relationship with Francis Bacon. There was no proof of strange-love matters, but such matters I abhorred. Common immorality 'twixt men and women was bad enough, but sodomy was quite another thing. Bacon, though of an intense brilliancy of mind, was not of a type to whom I wished to give a post of power. For all of this, he did give Essex good advice, sensible advice, I believe, but Essex ignored it as he ignored all words of wisdom.

★ ★ ★

Meanwhile, I had allowed Drake to take ship again in order to carry out a semi-piratical enterprise against the Spaniards. He was in joint command with Hawkins, sailing out of Plymouth in August 1595. From the first, the cousins did not agree, so that in effect, each commanded a separate fleet.

Interviewing them at Windsor, I ordered them to be back in nine months. They looked astounded.

'Well?' I cried impatiently. 'Why do you open your eyes so wide?'

Drake bowed. 'Majesty,' he said, 'the date of our return depends upon the blessing of God. We cannot arrange such things.' He glanced for confirmation at his cousin Hawkins, who nodded anxiously.

'Pooh, pooh, pooh!' said I. 'You have your impudence, so to call upon the Almighty to cover your uncertain and frivolous answers. I shall expect you back next May, so Godspeed my brave knights. Do your best and trust in the Lord as I shall trust in you.'

I gave them my hands to kiss and watched them retreat backwards from my presence before turning back to my clavichord, now called Virginals in my honour. I began to sing and play a pretty ditty by William Byrd, for despite my age, my voice was clear and true and my fingers agile and able to race rapidly over the keys.

But Hawkins died at sea and Drake continued alone, taking Nombre de Dios once more and attempting to march to Panama, only to be forced back by the Spanish military, retreating to his ships with a great loss of men. At Porto Bello the dysentery was rife and many fell ill, including poor Drake himself. I heard that he rose from his sick-bed to don his armour that he might die like a soldier, and the very next day he breathed his last. Ah, 'twas right sad, and the whole of England mourned the great hero, especially the good folk of Plymouth whose Mayor he had been. Ay, 'twas great loss indeed. I had admired Drake greatly. It will be long before another of him arises. May his name live for ever.

Certes, Essex was not fit to take Sir Francis Drake's place, for all he thought himself so. Yet his ardour in endeavour and his enthusiasm in venture were very great and I esteemed these things in him. Still hoping to put them to England's service, I tolerated his difficult nature for longer than I would ordinarily have done, feeling even then, that I would be able to train him as I had done others. I said as much to Robert Cecil when I let Essex go with my cousin Charles of Effingham as joint Commander of the Fleet in 1596.

'Have no fear Robert,' said I. 'I will break our young Essex of his will and pull down his great heart to learn service to others and to the realm.'

Cecil looked dubious and hunched his crooked shoulder in the way he had when his feelings were not in accord with mine. As it turned out, a great success came from Cadiz where two galleons were burned, two captured and Cadiz destroyed. This raised the military prestige of England high and added to the burdens of Spain in equal force. But 'twas Raleigh, not Essex, who managed the business of the galleons. Essex took it upon himself to burn the Spanish merchant ships in Cadiz harbour, thereby losing us a fortune.

At this news, Robert Cecil's face wore a look of ill-disguised triumph when he recounted it to me at Windsor, for he and his father detested Essex. With good reason too, for Essex was mortal jealous of their power and their friendship with me, doing all he could, in sly ways, to wreck their schemes, so full of folly as he was!

'He has burned the merchant fleet?' I burst out, unbelieving. 'Is he run mad? Indeed, he doth lack reason and stability, Robert. He becometh more of a liability than an asset! Come, there is more; I can tell it by your smug face. What is it? What fresh enormity has his Lordship perpetrated?'

And while the birds twittered in the quiet woods and the river Thames lapped gently by between its grassy banks, Cecil told me that Lord Essex had failed to intercept the Spanish plate-fleet, while the loot already taken had been stolen by deserters and sold. I was so furious that almost I lost my breath. I had laid out £50,000 in this enterprise and near all of it was gone. Shaking my fist under little Cecil's elegant nose, I let forth such a string of my choicest naval oaths that he fell back amazed.

'Shocked, are you?' I roared. 'Well, so am I, may God damn Lord Essex to bloody, poxy perdition! Is there more? There is? Well, tell me — let us have it all!'

Looking nervous, as well he might. Cecil stammered out that Lord Essex had created more knights. Jesu, would the boy never learn? There must be somewhat in him worth the harnessing, I hoped, and because he was of my blood I resolved to persevere a little longer with him, though 'twas hard enough going, no force.

So the next year, albeit with much misgiving, I allowed him on a fresh venture. Oh, how I missed my dear, precious Rob! He had been ambitious, ay, but he wished to please me; he had been hot-at-hand, but he loved me, and ah, I had loved him beyond any other. Sore did I feel the absence of sweet Kit Hatton who was so true and who had loved me. There was none now to love me as a man loves a woman. We were all too old, see'st thou. Why, I was nearing sixty-four, and looked it too, when not in company. Sure, I could still fettle myself up finely and still surpass the best through sheer force of majesty, splendour and will, when the effort was needed. But effort it was becoming nowadays, when in former times 'twas all pleasure. Although my wretched face was wrinkled, my bosom was still smooth, fair and white. I felt that to be most unjust, for a bosom may be covered while a face is in the open for all to gawk at. So I took to wearing gowns of exceeding low cut, to draw the eyes away from my countenance to my bosom. From the way the eyes lingered thereon, my ruse may have succeeded, but I doubt it, for mayhap those eyes were startled at such expanse of bosom upon so elderly a dame! Well, I know not and I care not. My fussy physician moaned to me that to eat such a mort of sweetmeats would finish off what teeth yet remained to me. I told him to go and boil his head for a pudding; that it was my pleasure to eat comfits and that I would continue so to do! Ay, and I got the poxy gout in my thumb, too, so why should I not comfort myself with sugarmeats? I knew full well, in my heart, that the pain was gout, but would not have it so, even though I could not use my hand to sign letters. Nay, it did not ache, 'twas not the gout, it *dare* not be the gout; not for Elizabeth Tudor! But it kept me from sleeping and nigh made me weep, for all my brave words and tight lips.

Eh, but I was thinking of Lord Essex and his mischiefs while on his next expedition. A mere six years agone that was, in 1597, and it seems at once but a se'ennight yet a lifetime away. His mission was to annihilate Spanish Philip's new Armada at Ferrol. I gave him instructions that were child-like in their clarity. He was to break up the Aramada, and only after that was he to sail for the Azores to hunt the treasure ships. This time 'twas not booty I wanted; I wished the new Armada blown off the seas. But his Lordship did not take Ferrol, nor the Armada, for he felt that his men were too badly weakened by the foul weather, so instead of obeying me he sailed for the Azores. Apparently his men were not too sick for that! When he got there he missed the treasure ships! I could not believe such idiot bungling — 'twas against all sense, all reason.

When he returned in October, I raged at him before the entire Court. 'Dost realise, thou conceited windbag, that we in England are lucky to have escaped attack from the very Armada that you were sent to destroy?' I bellowed. 'We were not protected by any of *your* doing, my Lord! Nay, 'twas the weather that held the Diegos back. That and that only! You are useless to me! Whatever you undertake, you botch!'

White with fury, he bowed rigidly and backed out of the Audience Chamber dangerous fast. He then refused to attend Court or Parliament in his angry sullenness. I was beginning to find him more nuisance than he was worth, I promise you. Naught but silence was heard from his direction until I gave my cousin Charles of Effingham the Earldom of Nottingham, which he richly deserved. Then what howls of protest sounded from Lord Essex! He was scorned, slighted, passed-over, put-upon, and I know not what all. This was desperate annoyance, for France and Spain seemed to be making a peace, and I wanted no internal strife to upset England's solidarity if there were to be negotiations.

So I was obliged to forgive Lord Essex yet again, though for political reasons only. It was very worrisome; I knew not what to do with this over-mettlesome gent. My dear old Burghley tried to warn him the next summer, sick and weak though he was growing at seventy-seven years of age. He tottered into my chamber at White Hall, fresh from a Council meeting, up-held by two sticks and a page, trembling in his furred robe, even though 'twas bright Maytime, his face creased with concern.

'Sit ye down, my dear good friend,' I bade him. 'What ails you that your face is so long?'

As he fumbled with his sticks, the page and I aided him to a cushioned settle. When we were alone he shook his head sadly from side to side, seeming worried and depressed. 'What ails you, Burghley?' I repeated loudly, for he was growing very deaf.

'Why, 'tis Lord Essex, Madam,' he replied heavily. 'He is wild war-monger, and I told him so. 'You breathe naught but war, slaughter and blood, my Lord,' said I. Then I passed my psalter across the table to him, open at the 25th Psalm, and pointed to verse 23, Madam.'

'Ah, I know it,' I answered. ' *'The bloody and deceitful men shall not live out half their days.'* What said he to that?'

'He understood me not,' replied Burghley. 'He is of no more use to you, Madam, than a quartan fever or an uncracked louse.'

Not only had Essex not heeded Burghley's warning, but had written an inflammatory letter to Anthony Bacon, brother to Francis, calling for outright war, and had the letter circulated for all to read. I was furious beyond words to describe, and took my Lord explosively to task in my Privy Chamber at Windsor, on the first day of July, in a most horrid scene. We yelled ourselves nigh hoarse, and then, upon my soul, he turned his back upon me! This gesture of contempt to a Sovereign was punishable by imprisonment at the least. In a flame, I flew at him and fetched him a woundy, great crack over each ear, and by Jesu, he actually laid his hand upon his sword! He could have been 'headed for that, no force!

'My God!' he shouted. 'I would not have taken such a thing even from your father!'

Well, he knew not my father.

Before I could hit him again, my arm being lifted to do so, Cousin Charles rushed between us, and with the help of others, forced Lord Essex through the door still roaring threats and vengeance at the top of his voice. Within the hour came the most saucy and insolent letter it has ever been my misfortune to receive, and my ire knew no bounds. I began to realise that at the age of well-nigh sixty-five, I was growing too old to contain such a mad-head. I could not turn to my precious Burghley, for he was sore ill and lame, having to be carried everywhere, and at the end of July he took to his bed. I was desolate upset and feared for him, hovering at his bedside, feeding him soup and gruel with mine own hand, day after day, endeavouring to hide my tears under a bright countenance. But he died, he died. On the 4th of August 1598, my beloved, invaluable, irreplaceable Burghley died. Fifty years agone he had come quiet to my help, aiding me when all was against me, and for forty of those fifty years he had been at my side in every way; honoured, loved, respected and trusted by me. No Sovereign had ever a more faithful servant, no woman a truer, more selfless friend.

With his death, I knew that my last

link with the past had been broken. I felt myself adrift upon a raging torrent of time, surrounded by those who knew and understood me not, separated from me by reason of their youth and different outlook upon life. 'Twas ghastly sensation; almost I wished to follow Burghley there and then. But I had to continue while God willed it, ageing and tiring though I was. Nay, I was not one to give up. I would fight to the end. But Burghley! Even now I weep if his name be mentioned, for in his way, he was more to me than any other. Ay, he was in some sort a father to me, my cherished Burghley.

And before that August was out, to add to my heaviness, there was a terrible battle at Yellow Ford in Ireland, where our English army was utterly routed. A dreadful, fearful year was 1598 . . .

Ireland. I was at my wits end over that country. There seemed to be no way of governing or aiding it. Its problems had occupied years of my time, to little effect, and always when a solution appeared to be nearing, somewhat would occur to wreck it. Such odd and strange doings took place there, 'twas no understanding them. English heads were turned, orders lost or disobeyed, extraordinary actions taken. Why, in 1597, I mind that I actually received the severed head of an Irish rebel chieftain as a gift! 'Twas of Fiach McHugh, unfortunate creature, and sent me by Thomas Lee, a presumptuous, scoundrelly captain who must have had maggots for brains. I was right disgusted at such behaviour and ordered the head sent back to Ireland to be decently bestowed. Such horrid, barbarous gift I never beheld. I near puked.

There had been rising after rising all through my reign, and none could decide how to rule Ireland, for all went awry as soon as the place was reached, as if some evil spell were at work there. Moreover, few of the Irish could speak English, uttering only in Erse, a tongue, which when I heard it, sounded like naught but hollering and howling. 'Twas from Shane O'Neill I heard it spoke, in 1562 at my Court, when I was but a young woman. Mind, he was a clever man, learning to speak English quick enough and clear enough for any to understand. I made him Earl of Tyrone in later years, thinking him our friend, but nay, he made treaties with the Spaniards against us. 'Twas his victory at Yellow Ford. Although I was ever inclined to peace rather than war, I was high enangered over this battle. I thought the whole business base and monstrous and wrote a fulminating letter to the Lords governing in Dublin, berating them for their rash insolency in allowing matters to get so out of hand uncontrolled.

I knew that a battle must be fought, it was the only way. But oh, the monies it would take! England could ill-afford such a drain. Robert Cecil and I agonised over it. My armies in Ireland were grown as crooked as corkscrews, the captains pocketing their pay while staying well away from any action. Young Will Shakespeare, the actor and playwright whom I had met as a boy long ago, had writ a most comical piece about my villainous captains, called *The Merry Wives of Windsor*. I near laughed myself silly over the antics of Sir John Falstaff, who was the personification of all my captains in one ruffianly knight. The play was most devilish apt and witty, and I was grateful to young Will for the relief of laughter in the midst of such fret and vexation.

It was urgently necessary for me to find a Commander-in-Chief for my forces in Ireland. No one wanted the post. Raleigh who was a-building and remaking Sherborne Abbey as his home, wanted none of Ireland, recommending me to have Tyrone murdered, for it would be no disgrace, he wrote. I refuted this idea at once, suggesting to my Council that Sir Charles Blount take command. This caused such great arguments that I put forward the name of Sir William Russell, but he flat refused, saying that he wished to live out his appointed time and not meet his end bewitched and corpsed in a peat-bog.

After the stormy scene I had had with Essex. I had warned him most severely about his violence and bad behaviour and, as ever, he had responded with tears, self-recriminations, regrets and sobbed-out promises. Weary of these recurrent dramatics, I hoped he meant his words, and indeed he seemed to do so, for the nonce, anyhap. I hoped the improvement would last. In default of any other for Commander in Ireland, and with the direst apprehension, I chose his Lordship for the post. To soothe my misgivings, I marshalled, in my mind, the facts in his favour.

Item: He was very wealthy. *Item*: He was a prime man of the nobility. *Item*: He had power and was in favour with military men. *Item*: He had led an army. *Item*: He could draw men, almost against themselves, to his side.

I pondered it long and grave that winter at White Hall. 'Twas a heavy matter. At last I decided that it should be Essex's chance to redeem himself, to prove that he had left his follies behind, that his nature had settled and grown into that of a man rather than of a spoiled child. He seemed to understand this — but when did Essex ever show his true self? I doubt if he himself knew it. At anyrate, he did understand that if he proved successful, he would be the greatest man in the land. But as soon as he reached Ireland in the April of 1599, he was writing complaining and angry letters to me about Raleigh having wished him ill-success and having spoken slightingly of him while he was not by to refute such words.

Such nonsense I never heard! Walter Raleigh had no reason to wish him ill, for Raleigh possessed large estates in Ireland. Essex wrote again, saying that Cecil wished him ill. Why so? Had not Cecil nigh worn himself out in the raising of money to finance the venture? I tossed these missives aside with a snort, far more angered to discover that he had acted against my wishes and had chosen the Earl of Southampton as his cavalry commander for no better cause than that of friendship. Friendship, indeed! I had deep doubt about that friendship, of its manner and closeness. I neither liked nor trusted Lord Southampton. He had married Eliza Vernon against my express desire, and I suspected him of being more than adaptable in his bodily urges, moreover. He was as happy to bed with a man as with a woman, and 'faith, he looked womanish enough! If I had been Mistress Vernon, I would not have given him a tumble, not I. Too many of Essex's friends were of this backside-forward persuasion and I mistrusted all such; 'twas foible of mine. I wrote to Essex, outraged at such disobedience in so important a matter.

Nor was this all. He was handing out knighthoods once more, and to rascally fellows who warranted not the honour. Soon his army would consist of tag and rag, cut and longtail, deserving only contempt from all. Besides he was flouting my known and most clear orders over how to conduct the campaign. He had been told to push north to Ulster at once, and engage Tyrone immediately. He did not, being dissuaded by the Council at Dublin, the members of which held no land in the North and so felt no interest in Ulster. So Essex moved through Leinster and Munster instead, finding but little opposition. Returning to Dublin with half his men sick of fevers and gripes, he then discovered his supplies to have run dangerously short.

By August, his army was of less than half its original strength. To my anxious letters he replied blaming his officers and men, which I thought shameful and craven indeed.

'It is disgraceful, disgusting!' I railed to Cecil. 'Oh, that I were a man and able to fight at the head of my army! And I would too — none so valiant! Essex is naught but a wretched *fainéant* with neither valour nor honour. Oh, that I could go to Ireland as a man and meet him there! I would make him pay and pay again for such betrayal of his country and me!'

I wrote Essex some searing letters, like to burn his eye-balls as he read the words. He had wasted fine men and good money, degraded his honour and mine, all by wilful, nigh insane, mismanagement and disobedience. He had given posts of high command to young gentlemen who rather desired to do well than knew how to perform it, and this when good strategy and firm action were vital. Already Tyrone was blazing his own triumphs to the whole of Europe. I counted Essex as defeated, I wrote, as so did all who were not in Ireland with him.

At last he obeyed and marched north. His letter reached me nigh on my sixty-sixth birthday. What a sweet gift it was *not*! Out tumbled the moanings and whinings. *His army was too weak and Tyrone's was too strong. He saw not how he could accomplish a victory in such case* . . . Great God, I wrote him a scathing answer, sending it off at once. Two days later came Captain Lawson to tell me that Essex had once again disobeyed instructions and had met the Earl of Tyrone in a parley. A pretty parley! Tyrone was as untrustworthy as Essex was unreliable, so naught but curds and turds could come of that. 'Twas insupportable. I knew naught of what had been said in this parley, nor of any instructions for a truce. A truce! It was beyond belief. I wrote instantly, commanding Essex to make sure that Tyrone should agree to have English garrisons stationed throughout his lands and to come to Court himself to make peace, or the precious truce was worth naught. I would grant nothing until the terms of this truce had been explained to me in detail and my permission obtained for all parts of it.

The answer to my letter arrived, in person, at Nonsuch Palace on Michaelmas Day, bursting wildly into my bedchamber at ten o'clock of the morning. I but newly risen, sat wrapped in a pink velvet bedgown, my white hair about my face. I was astounded, for here was my Lord Essex — who should have been about my business in Ireland — kneeling filthy-dirty and begrimed at my feet, frantically kissing my hands with his muddy lips, babbling of 'love' and 'forgiveness'! I said but little to him then, my mind being too busy to discover the safety of my palace and indeed my Kingdom.

After dinner I sent for him and began to call him to question for his return. 'I am not satisfied with you, my Lord,' I said, eyeing him coldly. 'How dare you come away so, in such manner, leaving all things at such great hazard? You may say whatever you have to say to the Lords of the Council at once. Come, my Lords! The Earl of Essex is here. Take him with you and question him close.'

Later that evening, I gave the order that Essex should keep his chamber and forbear to mix with any of the Court. I had with me at Nonsuch but four Privy Councillors, namely Robert Cecil, my cousin Henry of Hunsdon, Lord North and Sir William Knollys, so I sent out messages for more to come to me to talk over the shameful business. Upon the next day, after dinner was eaten, Lord Essex was called to appear before the Council, told to take off his hat and to remain standing whilst Cecil read out the charges against him that Cecil and I had compiled. For five long hours did the Lords have him under question, and in fifteen little minutes they concluded that he should be put under arrest.

I fretted over this all night and all the next day, the last of September, walking solitary in the park and gardens, staring absently at the carven, turreted facade of my father's fanciful dream in plaster, glass and stone; Nonsuch, glittering against the blue sky, bowered in trees. I saw it not, being busy with my heavy problem.

The next day I gave Essex into the custody of my Lord Keeper, Sir Thomas Egerton, at York House. He was sent off without ceremony, in a coach belonging to Lord Worcester, allowed but two servants and no visitors, not even his wife. Withindoors he was to stay; no walking in the garden, for who knew of what plots and plans or attempts to escape that might be made? For sooth, he had lost all of my respect and my trust. I could not employ him as a servant of the state, and I doubted that he would be content to remain a private gentleman. Mayhap a little stringency at York House would cool his rash and foolish brain.

But I still had some family affection for him, for when I heard near unto Christmastide, that he had the running belly-gripes and a fever, I sent my doctors to him with a recipe for my particular remedy;

my special broth made with herbs, wine and arrowroot, excellent for a flux of the bowels. I did not wish to see him again, nor to speak with him, but neither did I wish to break him by reason of a public trial, for I felt not vengeful, nor wishful to show him to all as he was. He had done most of that for himself.

In the springtime of 1600 I allowed him to go to Essex House, but with no state, a handful of servants only, and under the guardianship of Sir Richard Berkeley who was to retain all the keys. I wished Essex to have time to consider, and mayhap try to retrieve a little of his position by time of the Grand Hearing in June. Tom Egerton advised him to apologise and admit my authority, but this he would in no wise do, crying that 'twas all my fault!

'The man is crazy!' said I, bewildered, to my cousin Henry's son, young Robert Carey. 'Does he run upon his doom that he acts so?'

Robbie shook his handsome, dark head. 'Indeed, 'tis a puzzle, dear Madam. Even his friends are deserting him, for he speaks nonsense and treason together. Knowest thou that Francis Bacon, himself, is to speak against him at the Grand Hearing?'

'Bacon!' quoth I. 'He gets out while the going is good, I see. Well, I blame him not. He wishes to save his own skin, for it seems that none can save Essex's. He puts all against him and runs blind and wilful to perdition. It is some twist in his head, Robbie. Mayhap 'twas always there.'

★ ★ ★

In August I made a foolish error. I allowed myself to listen to my heart. I gave Essex his freedom, but refused him a post or a place at Court. Ah, I know it. I should have kept him under house-arrest, but to treat mine own blood so! I had been forced to it with Queen Marie and 'twas against my deepest feelings. Also, if it should be that Robert Cecil's party became too powerful, Essex would serve as a counter-balance, so my head was in it — a little.

He was fathoms deep in debt and had the impudence to write me begging letters for money to pay the shiftless swarms of knights and captains who filled his house. He could not pay them, he said, for the monopoly I had granted him on sweet wines had run out with the beginning of the new century, thus removing the greater source of his income. I did not renew the monopolies, neither. As a result of this, I heard that he had roared out: 'The Queen's mind is as crooked as her carcase!'

This did not endear him to me nor make me relent to his cause. Next, I heard of weird and fantastical plots that he was hatching, and a few months later there was news of a desperate scuffle in the road outside Durham House between Lord Southampton and Lord Grey, in which a poor young page lost a hand and near died of it. This convinced Lord Essex that I had made a plot for Lord Grey to kill him. Certes, his mind was turning, for sure. Mayhap he had contracted the French pox — it has bad effect on the brain. Who could tell? He was like none I ever knew.

'Twas Walter Raleigh warned me of a rebellion, coming to me all aghast at White Hall, but a month after. It was cold February and I was dancing a galliard with my ladies in the gallery for warmth, all of us bundled in velvets and furs. Seeing the look on Sir Walter's face, I bade my ladies leave us and went to sit at the fireside drawing Raleigh with me, by the hand.

'What ails you, my Walter?' I asked. 'Is it bad news of Essex?'

'The worst, Madam,' he replied, his dark eyes sharp with worry. 'There is a plot to capture White Hall and force you to have Lord Grey and his friends executed. It seems that Essex would constrain you, in some sort, Madam.'

I was incredulous. Indeed, I almost laughed. ' 'Tis he must be constrained,' I said. 'Restrained, too. I must inform the Council.' And a meeting was held at once, Secretary John Herbert being sent to bring Essex back with him for a full explanation.

Essex refused to accompany John Herbert, saying he was 'afeard for his life, to leave his house.'

'Good God!' I cried. 'It is Norfolk all over again! What sweet relatives have I that would plot against their kinswoman and Queen!'

Before the sun was up of the next day, Raleigh took a boat down-river to a secluded place, close to the watergate of Essex House, where he met Lenna von Snakenburg's second husband, the Devonian-born Sir Tom Gorges who had become entangled with Essex and wished himself out of it. Rowing swiftly back to White Hall, Raleigh had me roused, begging to speak with me at once.

Clapping on my wig, I poked my head through the bed-curtains, blinking sleepily. 'What now?' I expostulated. 'Is Essex under my bed that you would have me out of it so summary?'

'Jest not, Madam,' he beseeched. 'I have

seen Tom Gorges who says there is to be a bloody day of it. Already I have been shot at from the river bank by one of Essex's men. They mean to rouse the City and inflame the apprentices.'

'Oh Jesu!' I groaned. 'Will his foolishness never end? Go now, Water-Walter — I will be out of my chamber yarely. All will be well.'

Calling my tire-women, I had them dress me quick while I formulated a plan. I sent Egerton, with a group of Lord Essex's friends and relatives, to Essex House to persuade him, if they could, against violence. Meanwhile, I ordered another group of noblemen to call up soldiers and advance on Essex House. I sent an urgent message to the Lord Mayor and the Aldermen before eight o'clock of the morn, to warn them to keep the City calm. Then I ate a manchet of bread, two handsful of marchpane fruits and drank a cup of good ale before continuing with the business of the day. I had no real doubt of the outcome, but did not seek slumber that night until I had heard that Lord Essex was taken after a mighty chase-about.

He had had Egerton and his company locked into Essex House and had rushed out with a large band of armed men, making

261

for the City, to harangue the people as they left St. Paul's after worship that Sunday, but was too late, for the churchgoers had all gone home. He then hurried off to his friend Sheriff Smythe's house in Fenchurch Street. But Smythe would have none of any rebellious plot, running out of the back door of his own house, straight to that of the Lord Mayor and blurting out the whole. Essex thereupon stayed three hours in Smythe's house, eating a goodly dinner, while my soldiers made for the City and while his own men deserted him. Amazed at this, Lord Essex raced to the riverside where he commandeered boats to take him and his remaining followers back to Essex House stairs, there to find that Tom Gorges had freed those trapped in the house, and that the place itself was surrounded by troops. Creeping up the water-stairs into the garden, he and Southampton were at once taken. They spent part of the night across the water in Lambeth Palace and, at three o'clock of the next morning, were taken swift to the Tower.

'And I should think so!' said I from my bed, where I rested propped up against a mound of pillows. 'God's wounds, I never heard the like. It resembles a tale made up for a child. Well done, Egerton. All went as smooth as grease, I can tell, despite your imprisonment in Essex House! Give my praise to whom it is due, for I swear my eyes are closing of themselves. What an almighty shuffle over naught but moonshine and fantasies. 'Tis beyond credit.'

★ ★ ★

I was weary of the whole stupid, dangerous nonsense, but still ready to listen to reason, if any there was in it, when a day or so after all the garboil, a man was captured right in White Hall Palace and close to my private rooms. He meant no good, neither. I had myself dressed in one of my richest gowns, thus to awe him, and had him brought to me. It was Captain Thomas Lee. I viewed him with marked disfavour.

'What is he about?' I asked of those who held him.

'Why Majesty, he says he was to burst in upon you at your supper and compel you to sign a release for Lord Essex.'

'*Compel* me?' I thundered. 'This dog thinks to compel his Queen? Upon my soul, what next? Thomas Lee, now that I see you, I like you no better than I did some years agone when the bloody head of an Irish chieftain fell at my feet out of a bag of your sending. How dare you lend yourself to plots against me? How dare you seek to use force against me? You shall be tried at Newgate, and I dare swear your head may well leave your own shoulders! Take him away!'

He was executed three days after, the nasty fellow. His nose were better out of Lord Essex's business, or it would not have hit the scaffold. What times, what times!

I was not at the trial of the Lords Essex and Southampton at Westminster on the 19th of February. I wished not to see it, but I heard that the two Lords postured, jeered, sniggered and smirked throughout, seeming to care for naught, all through the nine hours of the trial, ceasing to titter and giggle only when found guilty on every charge. That wiped the grins from their faces. So much so, that within two days Lord Essex confessed all, showing himself most hatefully and ignobly ready to speak against all the friends who had been with him in the plot, and willing to lay information against those not yet called in question! What a vile and craven heart to beat in such a comely body. What a spiteful spirit to work in such a handsome head! It was right saddening to know.

Well, he was not worth the saving. Of the eighty-six brought for trial, only six were executed and thirty-two I allowed to go quite free. Lord Southampton I spared also. His poor mother pleaded for him in agony of tears and supplication. I felt much sympathy for her sorrow and for her having so wormish a son. I believed he had been led astray, which was true, for he was full weak and easy influenced. Cecil too, thought he might be spared as he had been naught but a silly waxen image in Essex's hands, while his brain, with guidance, might be set to productive work.

I hated, of all things, to kill. 'Twas against my whole nature. But there was no other end possible for Essex, even though I was reluctant to sign the death warrant, tearing one up once I had signed it. Yet I steeled myself in the end, and he went to the scaffold at eight of the morning on the 25th of February 1601, dying at the first stroke of the axe. God be thanked there was no bungling.

8

THE CASE IS ALTERED
1601 – 1603

So the months and days rolled on. Money was short; the Irish war had seen to that. There was trouble over the monopolies when a member of Parliament called monopolies 'the bloodsuckers of the Commonwealth' with many other members in noisy agreement. In fact, Robert Cecil's government could not control Parliament upon this question, and I had to take the reins myself, issuing a proclamation abolishing many monopolies. I told my Parliament that I would see a deputation of members about it at White Hall.

'A deputation only? Nay! All, all, all!' they cried vociferously, stamping their feet with clamorous good-humour.

'Come ye then, if the chamber will hold you!' I answered, laughing. 'I will see ye all, all, all, at three o'clock of the afternoon of the last day of November in the Council Chamber at the palace. So until then, good sirs, fare ye well.' And I left to the sound of resounding cheers.

'Well, I spoke them full and fair upon the appointed day. My Golden Speech they called it. I recall most of it too, for 'twas not made so long ago.

' . . . God hath raised me high,' I said, 'yet this I count the glory of my crown, that I have reigned with your loves . . . Neither do I desire to live longer days than I may see your prosperity, and that is my only desire . . . Yea, mine own properties I account yours to be expended for your good. Rise up gentlemen!' I cried. 'Kneel no more, for I am grateful to you for showing me this abuse of monopoly . . . I could give no rest unto my thoughts until I had reformed it . . . I know I am only a woman and unworthy, but God hath give me strength and a heart that never feared any home or foreign enemy . . . I attribute nothing to myself, 'tis the doing of Providence. For I, oh Lord, what am I, whom practices and perils past should not forbear? Or what can I do? That I should speak for any glory, God forbid! And now that I have done, sirs, will ye bring to me all those who wish to kiss my hand before they depart to their neighbourhoods?'

I thought they would never stop their shouting and felt great love and friendship for them. It might be the last Parliament I would see, at sixty-eight, I reasoned, and I gave them my best. I am glad I did ay, glad I did . . .

E'en so short a time ago I was in command of all my faculties. Now decay crumbles me, nibbling at brain and body. Ah, soon, soon must I take to my bed, for a creeping chill is upon me and my power even to remain crouched upon these cushions will be spent . . .

★ ★ ★

Upon the Eve of Christmas, but a se'ennight after my last Parliament, Lord Mountjoy won a victory over the Earl of Tyrone and the Spanish forces stationed in Ireland. The Diegos surrendered and Tyrone fled, not to be found for nigh on a year, wily fellow that he was, knowing his shaggy, boggy country like a map as he did.

I was still well and hardy, excellent disposed to hunting, being every second day a-horseback and continuing long thereon. I still enjoyed bear-baiting — my favourite bears, Harry Hunks, Great Ned and Sackerson were yet stout and fierce fighters. Indeed, I owned the Paris Garden Bear Pit at Southwarke and relished many visits there, riding upon one or other of my two favoured mounts, Grey Poole or Black Wilford. And I saw many a fine play performed too — eleven in a season, I believe it was — some at Placentia, some at White Hall. I loved a good play.

Ay, I was still in health. Why, only last August, but seven months back, did I ride a full ten miles and then go a-hunting on the same day! That was nigh unto my sixty-ninth birthday. And after that, on Ascension Day, when the bells rang and we had the customary tilting at White Hall, my fool Garret made us near to split a-laughing as he pranced about on a little small pony no bigger than a good ban-dog. Why my yellow mastiff with the black ears was the larger, I'll swear!

And at Christmas I dined at Robert Cecil's fine new mansion in the Strand and well-enjoyed me, yet in leaving did I slip on the step and strain my foot, pest take it. It aches a little, e'en now. Then there was a feast at my cousin Henry of Hunsdon's house, and another at that of my other cousin Charles of Nottingham. 'Twas all delightful. I saw more plays ay, and I danced at the Twelfth Night revels. Ah, 'twas upon that Twelfth Night that I began to think and remember. Yea, to remember myself as a little wean of two or three years . . . ay, and all of my life thereafter. A long,

long life. A marvellous life. Watched over, guarded and guided by God Who disposes all things. He brought me through trials to power and glory unimaginable. He held me high to raise my England as high. He saved me long enough to impress the Venetian Ambassador but six weeks agone with a brave show which was to be my last.

I sparkled then, so little a while back, I shone, I shed my radiance around as I have ever known how to do. I spoke to the Ambassador in Italian, in Latin, in Greek; I showed him that my knowledge and grasp of political affairs were as sharp and hard as ever. An ageless goddess, shimmering with jewels, I seemed. Gloriana, ever-young, they said. Ay, 'twas my last show. It tired me nigh unto death, see'st thou. Nigh unto death, where I remain, mute upon that shadowy threshold.

Now I hunch upon my cushious here at Richmond and the case is altered with me. Ay, for my time is done. I know I am like to die . . . . It is the 21st of March, I believe, and pretty spring begins shyly to smile. New life buds all around my windows as mine draws to its close.

What is it that my ladies are saying? What do they say?

'Pray, pray go to bed, dear your Majesty,' they say.

'Where is Kate? Where is my cousin?' I mutter. But before they can answer I remember. She is dead some weeks since and poor Charles is widower.

'Delphy?' I croak.

She is there. She comes to me, pleading for me to go to bed.

'Mayhap, mayhap . . . ' I mumble. Then, feeling faint: 'Ay.'

* * *

So they undress me and carry me to my great bed in my bedchamber at dear, rosy Richmond. Well, I do feel a little better, ay, just a little better . . .

'Meat broth.' I say. It comes and it is good. Good . . .

I am dying.

I cannot speak. I turn from one side to the other. I cannot speak. I am dying.

Now I lie still, upon my right side. My feet are cold. I am dying.

Rob? Rob? Is it you? Nay, 'tis Delphy asking to read to me. So she reads some meditations in a soft, clear voice.

I am dying.

Who are these about my bed? Shadows?

271

Spirits? Nay, nay, I know them. I see Cousin Charles, Tom Egerton, and there at the bed's foot stands little Robert Cecil. What say they?

'Dear Madam, trouble ye not to speak. Do but raise your hand if you agree to our proposals.'

Proposals? What proposals? . . . Ah, the Succession . . . Yea, the Succession . . .

'Dearest Madam, is King James of Scotland to follow you?'

It has come. I must answer. No escaping it now.

I raise my hand.

It is done. Little King James will be King of England. 'Tis only right and fair. Her son, Marie's son. 'Tis only fair . . .

More shadows come to me. They are Archbishop Whitgift and dear young Robbie Carey. Others are near; I hear their breathings and rustlings. Weeping. Now they pray. They pray for me because I am dying.

It is the 23rd of March and I am dying.

Now there is naught but sobs and silence. I like it not. I would have more prayers to ease my leaving. Oh, my dear beloved England, farewell, farewell . . .

Where is Delphy? I cannot speak. I raise my hand and Delphy's sweet face swims into my dim and fading view.

'You wish more prayers, dearest?' she says. Such kind perception as she has. I flutter my hand again, and soon I hear the sonorous sound of Whitgift's voice above a chorus of others repeating the beautiful words. I hear sobs. No use to sob. I cannot return. My legs are cold, for I am dying.

Still the voices echo in my chamber. Soothing, soothing, comforting, beautiful . . .

They have stopped. Why so? Wearily I raise my fingers just a little and the chanting begins again. 'Mercy, mercy, mercy dear God, for our precious Queen,' they pray. 'Receive her into Thine arms, O Lord of Heaven and Earth.'

My heart is cold, Oh, I am dying.

It is dark, dark . . . For a long time it is dark and cold . . .

I see my Rob! My darling, my love, you are here. *Come, beloved,* says he. *Come and love me.* And I rise. Yea, I rise, all young and beautiful and go to him . . .

There is Burghley, my Spirit. He is with me. My sister, weeping, floats by; my brother is beside me. And beside me too, is my precious Kat. So long a time between, Kat! Stay, stay close . . .

Oh, my father! Father, do you smile upon me? What is it you say? *Well done, my brave and gallant daughter. Braver and more gallant than I*, you say. Father, Father . . . Father, Rob, Kat, Burghley . . . Mother? . . . Here is Bess.

Elizabeth Tudor is no more. She is gone.

NOW SPEAKETH SIR JOHN HARINGTON, GODSON TO THE QUEEN
24th March 1603

Ay, she is gone. At a quarter-to-three upon the morning of the Assumption of the Blessed Virgin. She departed this life mildly like a lamb, easily, like a ripe fruit dropping from a tree; softly as the most resplendent sun setteth in a western cloud.

There were few who did not love her, dear, wondrous, extraordinary, fantastical, marvellous Queen. Gloriana was she well named. There have been none like her before, nor will there be yet to come. She *was* England. Her memory will never die so long as England shall live.

When she smiled, it was pure sunshine that everyone did choose to bask in if they could, while anon would come a sudden gathering of the clouds and great was the thundering thereof. Yet after this, all would shine again and be merry.

She was a Queen who hath so long, and with such great wisdom governed her

Kingdom, that the like hath not been read or heard of either in our time or since the days of Rome. England's Queen and saviour has gone, but she will live in the hearts of men for ever.

THE END

We do hope that you have enjoyed reading this large print book.

Did you know that all of our titles are available for purchase?

We publish a wide range of high quality large print books including:
Romances, Mysteries, Classics, General Fiction, Non Fiction and Westerns.

Special interest titles available in large print are:
**The Little Oxford Dictionary
Music Book
Song Book
Hymn Book
Service Book**

Also available from us courtesy of Oxford University Press:
**Young Readers' Dictionary
(large print edition)
Young Readers' Thesaurus
(large print edition)**

For further information or a free brochure, please contact us at:
**Ulverscroft Large Print Books Ltd.,
The Green, Bradgate Road, Anstey,
Leicester, LE7 7FU, England.
Tel:** (00 44) 0116 236 4325
Fax: (00 44) 0116 234 0205

HIJACK
OUR STORY OF SURVIVAL

Lizzie Anders and Katie Hayes

Katie and Lizzie, two successful young professionals, abandoned the London rat race and set off to travel the world. They wanted to absorb different cultures, learn different values and reassess their lives. In the end they got more lessons in life than they had bargained for. Plunged into a nightmarish terrorist hold-up on an Ethiopian Airways flight, they were among the few to survive one of history's most tragic hijacks and plane crashes. This is their story — a story of friendship and danger, struggle and death.

THE VILLA VIOLETTA

June Barraclough

In the 1950s, Xavier Leopardi returned to Italy to reclaim his dead grandfather's beautiful villa on Lake Como. Xavier's English girlfriend, Flora, goes to stay there with him and his family, but finds the atmosphere oppressive. Xavier is obsessed with the memory of his childhood, which he associates with the scent of violets. There is a mystery concerning his parents and Flora is determined to solve it, in her bid to 'save' Xavier from himself. Only after much sorrow will Edwige, the old housekeeper, finally reveal what happened there.

BREATH OF BRIMSTONE

Anthea Fraser

Innocent enough — an inscription in a child's autograph book; a token from her new music teacher, Lucas Todd, that had charmed the six-year-old Lucy. But in Celia, Lucy's mother, it had struck a chill of unease. They had been thirteen at table that day — a foolish superstition that had preyed strangely on Celia's mind. And that night she had been disturbed by vivid and sinister dreams of Lucas Todd . . . After that, Celia lived in a nightmare of nameless dread — watching something change her happy, gentle child into a monster of evil . . .

THE WORLD AT NIGHT

Alan Furst

Jean Casson, a well-dressed, well-bred Parisian film producer, spends his days in the finest cafes and bistros, his evenings at elegant dinner parties and nights in the apartments of numerous women friends — until his agreeable lifestyle is changed for ever by the German invasion. As he struggles to put his world back together and to come to terms with the uncomfortable realities of life under German occupation, he becomes caught up — reluctantly — in the early activities of what was to become the French Resistance, and is faced with the first of many impossible choices.